Cop Show Heaven

Lawrence Gray

Supported by

Hong Kong Arts Development Council

The Hong Kong Arts Development Council fully supports freedom of artistic expression. The views and opinions expressed in this project do not represent the stand of the Council.

Cop Show Heaven

A character in a popular cop show, Dan Symmonds, is written out of the series and finds himself lingering in Cop Show Heaven. Here he must try to discover some depth to his personality in order to inspire a writer to re-invent him.

But of course, that's just propaganda because no-body really wants depth, they just want what sells, or if not that, they just want that which sells what they want to sell! Here we are in a world aware of its own fictional nature, questioning the reasons for its own existence.

In this parody of parodies, any resemblance that Cop Show Heaven bears to Hong Kong and its film-making community is purely coincidental and whoever the readership assumes any of the characters to resemble is much mistaken. All is fiction. All is fantasy. Nothing is predicted. No thesis is proffered. No solution is offered. And it all ends as Hollywood would have it end, with a beginning. Shakespeare might hold up a mirror to the times, but Gray holds up a mirror to the mirror.

Lawrence Gray was born and educated in the UK and took BA honours in Economics and Politics from Leeds University. He has lived in Hong Kong since 1991. He is a professional screenwriter and director and has written episodes of UK and Singapore TV dramas and written, produced and directed a number of films in English and Cantonese. He directed the feature film "Lust $ Found", which he describes as an eccentric English gangster movie set in Hong Kong.

Gray's collection of short stories, *Odds and Sods*, was published in 2014 as a Proverse Prize Publication. It features stories that meld French farce, Chinese opera, religious mysticism, Hollywood and Hong Kong movies in a kaleidoscopic tour de force.

In Hong Kong he founded the Hong Kong Writers' Circle and chaired the group for twenty years, publishing many collections of stories from a wide variety of Hong Kong writers.

Gray has taught screenwriting in various cities around the world, and was one of the first to professionalize the industry. In 1996, he won the first Public Awareness of Science drama award (PAWS) and the Hong Kong-Asia Film Financing Forum's (HAF's) award for best Hong Kong film project of the year in 2006.

Cop Show Heaven

Lawrence Gray

Proverse Hong Kong

Cop Show Heaven
by Lawrence Gray.
2nd pbk edition pub. in Hong Kong by Proverse Hong Kong, January 2016
Copyright © Proverse Hong Kong, January 2016
ISBN: 978-988-8228-17-1
Printed by CreateSpace

1st published in pbk Hong Kong by Proverse Hong Kong,
9 April 2015.
Copyright © Proverse Hong Kong, 9 April 2015
ISBN: 978-988-8227-80-8

1st ed. distribution
(Hong Kong and worldwide):
The Chinese University Press of Hong Kong,
The Chinese University of Hong Kong, Shatin, NT, Hong Kong SAR.
E-mail: cup-bus@cuhk.edu.hk Web site: www.chineseupress.com
(United Kingdom):
Christine Penney, Stratford-upon-Avon, Warwickshire CV37 6DN,
England. Email: chrisp@proversepublishing.com

Distribution & other enquiries: Proverse Hong Kong, P.O. Box 259,
Tung Chung Post Office, Lantau, NT, Hong Kong SAR, China.
E-mail: proverse@netvigator.com; Web site: www.proversepublishing.com

Cover art by and with kind permission of Lawrence Gray.
Cover design, Artist Hong Kong Company. Page design, Proverse Hong Kong.

British Library Cataloguing in Publication Data.
A catalogue record for the 1st edition of this book is available
from the British Library.

Dedicated to that long-suffering patron of the arts,
my wife, Helen.

THE HOOK

"Right. This is what the writer got on you. So this is insider knowledge. And I'm giving it to you cos I likes you, brother. I don't do none of this for nobody else."

"You're bullshitting aren't you?"

"Hell, sure I am. But I'm God. I gotta at least seem all-merciful and benevolent. So listen up. Here's the word: A character in a popular cop show, Dan Symmonds, is written out of the series and finds himself lingering in Cop Show Heaven. Here he must try and discover some depth to his personality in order to inspire a writer to re-invent him.

"Cop Show Heaven came into existence because heaven rented part of hell to allow dead directors the pleasure of making movies – I mean, there ain't no conflict in heaven, so you can't do good movies in heaven. Right? Anyway, the Devil wants it back and is not allowing heaven to renew the lease ... Now that is a long story! But it ain't your problem. That's mine. So, you just gotta get with the programme and get on with it ...

"Now, where was I? Ah, yes: Lance Stirling, a dead director noted for making talking monkey movies, wants to make a serious flick about the handover and he casts Dan Symmonds – that's you – as the hero. Dan however, becomes embroiled with the family of one of the stuntmen, Fizzy Tang. Fizzy, seeing a future for Dan, wants him to seduce his ex-wife and take her away with him to the fabled land of Hollywood. He fears that if she does not go with Dan, she will forever have custody of his daughter, Lily. Dan however ... Oh, you don't need to know all this shit ..."

"Go on."

"No, I don't think I should do that. Otherwise you'll think it is all predestined."

"Isn't it?"

"You have choice."

"I'm a character out of a cop show, what choice do I have other than following the script?"

"You gotta behave as if you do have choice. If I give you the script, then how's that gonna look?"

"It's gonna ... going to look like I've learnt my part. That's what."

"But you ain't an actor. You is a character. There's a difference. The actor learns the part. You *is* the part. Right? Get it?"

"Oh."

"Jeremy Irons is an actor. And if you don't buck your ideas up, you're going to end up being played by him!"

"That's good? Not good?"

"That's where free will comes in."

CHAPTER ONE

In a dream I was snuffed out by a bullet fired from a gun in the hand of a minor character. I had thought I was doing well, that I was featuring in many stories, that my adventurous outlook was amusing the audience, but the actor who was playing me had better offers elsewhere, and the writer who wrote me had a sudden loss of faith in my personality. I would have liked to have seen the viewing figures and the letters of complaint, but it was too late, for once the audience no longer have you in mind, you fall through the clouds into their collective unconsciousness, "Cop Show Heaven."

So when I awoke I was in transit. The melatonin tablets had knocked me out, reset my time-clock, but still left me shell-shocked, with the unshaven wrecked expression of a man waking from a reality show. I looked at my fellow passengers, but nobody else appeared to exhibit my symptoms.

In a fug of exhaustion I staggered through immigration, obtained the visa stamp, and went on to collect luggage. The new world, I told myself, was my oyster, although I had heard that one should avoid oysters for fear of high cadmium content. Nevertheless, I declared myself prepared. The light at the end of the tunnel, or at least through the doors leading to the reception lounge, could be seen, and over the loudspeakers I could hear the tinkling of airy tunes. I was in a movie. Perfect! Death was impossible. Misery would end happily.

The electric doors opened and I made my entrance. I felt in my pocket for the business card that gave the name of my only contact. It was there. I was safe. All I needed to do was find that person and there would be bed and sustenance.

"Taxi?"

Before I could respond, my luggage was taken and I found myself following a dirty T-shirt.

"Aren't the taxis in that direction?"

"They are special taxis," said the man with a grin. It was the face of a young man with a very definite sort of haircut. It had been carefully sculptured so that an inch thickness of hair covered his head from the nape of his neck to his fringe. I hurried on ahead, pushing my way through idly chatting, baggily uniformed security guards.

"Are we going the right way?"

"This way this way," insisted the Haircut, scurrying over to a taxi with its boot open. Under a barrage of tooting horns, the Haircut threw my case into the trunk and opened the doors.

"This is quicker than queuing," he said. "You pay a hundred dollar now as fast lane tax."

I sorted through my money, found a crumpled red hundred-dollar note and sat back scowling.

"Where d'you want to go?" said the Haircut.

I fished out the business card, handed it over to the man, who studied it, then nodded, and turned the ignition. A smiling plastic doll jiggled on the dashboard.

I watched the city pass by in a swirl of curling concrete roads. Blue wooden trucks splattered with incomprehensible signs jostled for position.

"Don't you worry," shouted Haircut. "I'm not cheating you."

I found myself being driven slowly through hordes of pedestrians.

"I see handbags are in this season," I said, noticing how the smallest of people tended to carry the largest of bags.

"Huh?" said Haircut, as we swerved off the road up the driveway of a large grey concrete building. We stopped beside a scruffy artificial pond full of brown slimy water.

"Is this it?" I asked.

"Yep," he said with a scowl. I noticed that the pond was full of turtles piling upon one another, and handed over the money.

Haircut grinned and tossed a couple of small coins into the turtle pond, one of them hitting a turtle on the nose and sending its head sharply back into its shell.

"If you can't make it in Cop Show Heaven," he said, "you're a turtle."

*

I was in a dank corridor dangling with electricity cables above a row of metal mailboxes. A blast of conditioned air made me shiver as I walked to the elevators. I hoped to find a map explaining where I was but there was nothing.

The door opened and I saw myself reflected in a large mirror on the wall. I looked terrible.

I entered and as the doors closed I hit the second-floor button. Then quickly I spruced up the hair and ran fingers over the chin stubble.

The door opened on a dingy looking foyer closed off at either end by fire doors. It had the look of a multi-story car park, so I hit the third floor button. Again, the door opened upon a dingy looking foyer.

On floor eight, I glimpsed a little man in a dark suit holding a large watch.

"Excuse me!" I yelled.

The man ignored me, scuttled away, and turned at the end of the corridor. I ran after him and followed him into a men's toilet. The watch was not a watch; it was a compass.

"Excuse me?"

"Sorry," said the man, his eyes busily examining the surroundings. He took out a Cartier pen and scribbled something upon a notepad. Then he scrutinised the windows.

"Could you help me with this," I said, showing him the card.

The man examined me very closely.

"You come from far away," he said. "Everything is so easy and then it is not so easy."

"Well you got that right," I said, and the man nodded.

"You have a very stubborn forehead," said the man.

"Thank you."

"And a beautiful nose."

"But I'm looking for this person," I said.

"This is a city in transition," said the man, ignoring me. "It is gripped by uncertainty and fear. There are many dangers. Back to the mountain. Face to the sea. That is how one lives safely and prosperously. But they put a tunnel through the old mountain and let the cold wind through."

"So that's where the draught comes from?"

The man nodded, and preoccupied with his deep thoughts, left.

I followed him through the end doors and entered a corridor flanked by little offices. I could sniff the ink of photocopiers and although the notice-boards were incomprehensible, I knew this was the right place.

11

I looked in through the doors and waved my card.

"Ahem," I kept saying to draw attention. "Cop Show Heaven?"

I was eventually met with a look of recognition and a finger pointing across the corridor to a large and prosperous office with busy people in designer labels.

I pushed through the door and caught sight of a fat man sitting on a sofa in the waiting area. He was wearing a double-breasted suit with trouser turn-ups and reading a newspaper.

I had this sudden fear that when the newspaper was lowered, I would find myself staring at myself ten years on.

"Poland?" I enquired.

The man sat up straight and folded his paper.

"Yes?" he said.

"Sydney Poland?"

"Do I know you?"

I recalled last seeing him dressed in a lime-green body-stocking gathering in the natural energy during a breathing exercise. Could it have been so long ago that the ticket for this trip was bought?

"I doubt that you can remember me," I said. "But I once shared your character in an early draft."

Sydney folded up his paper, pulled out a silver cigarette case and carefully extracted a cigarette.

"Aah," he said. "So I was your master. How careless of me not to have a clue who the hell you are."

This was a test. All that I had to do was find the right word and Sydney would reveal some useful piece of information. Maybe I should give him a fond reiteration of Sydney's favoured inner-cleansing method, consisting of swallowing a long tape inch by inch over several days until it popped out of the arse whereupon one flossed the entire body clean. It was a brave fellow who thought a popular TV show would allow a middle-aged hero a penchant for esoteric practices.

"Are you still teaching?" I asked.

Suddenly the door beside Sydney swung open and a voice growled, "Sydney, you send the boy in."

"I wouldn't go in there if I was you," said Sydney. "Run away before it is all too late."

I peered through the door and saw an alarming woman with thick black eye make-up, wearing a lacy cocktail pants suit. She waved a folder before her.

"They call me the Dragon Lady," she growled, beckoning me forward.

The tightness and thinness of her pants gave her pubic region the prominence of a cricketer's box.

"Don't do it boy," whispered Sydney. "You'll never get away."

"I'm pure show-biz honey!" growled the Dragon Lady. "You must be Barry's friend. You're the big cop show star, only you're dead now. Isn't that it?"

"Well something like that," I said, still hesitating to venture through the door.

Sydney lit up his cigarette and flashed his eyebrows at me.

"You're Josephine, then?" I said, trying to be polite, though I seriously considered running away. Only the thought that she would sort out my accommodation and put me on the payroll kept me there.

"How's Barry doing?" she asked. "Such a pretty boy. Such an obliging young man."

Josephine giggled as she entertained herself with thoughts of past adventures. She was after all, pure show-biz.

"We had him as a punk rocker," continued Josephine eulogising the fun that was once Barry, "Everyone had him as a punk rocker. Every film made that month had Barry with his hair on end, Mohican, you know. Barry's body was so beautiful. And *what* talent! Such a waste! 'Barry,' I said, 'You should really get down to serious work and not this going here, going there, doing a bit of this, of that.' But some people have too much talent you know …"

Barry had been a gay lover in another draft and was always being written in and then hastily written out, as heroism always required heterosexuality. I assume he is swimming with the turtles now, despite script editors always loving his character. Serve him right for being an endearing one-dimensional stereotype.

I could not bear to listen to how wonderful Barry was, so I began to look crumpled and weary, hoping that would cue a cut to the chase. Josephine continued for some time outlining her qualifications for the job of casting director. She knew everyone, and knew talent when she saw it, was a connoisseur of character, and though disapproving of much of what she herself had done in the past, there was nothing else for a true artist but to get on with whatever was on offer. There is the rough and there is the smooth, and in Cop Show Heaven everyone has to do everything. That is the way of the world. One eats with one eye closed otherwise one does not eat at all.

"It's been a long journey," said Josephine, wistfully looking back upon a rich and varied life, and reaching for a folder containing some of the clippings of her highlights.

"Yes, yes," I said. "Who deals with my expenses?"

"Don't you worry," said Josephine, disappointed at not finding an audience for her clippings, but not surprised. "A talented boy like you. Friend of Barry's …"

"Who do I claim my expenses from?"

I had her on the run so decided to cross the threshold of her office. I would be pleasant later, even to the extent of looking over her clippings. Firstly, though, I had to get business out of the way. Josephine put aside her own folder and opened the file with my name and photograph plastered over the front.

"See," said Josephine, "we have everything ready. But we already cast all roles."

"That's not what I was told. Otherwise I would not have travelled all this way."

Josephine carefully replaced the file on the shelf of her office wall. Each of her fingers had a diamond ring and each nail was long and sparkling with golden glitter.

"Get yourself a room somewhere," she said. "Then let us know how to contact you."

"I was told you would sort it out," I said. "I'm sorry to press this point but I like everything clarified up front before I start working, otherwise I will be worried about it all the time."

With a deep sigh, Josephine pulled a bottle of brandy from her drawer.

"Would you like a drink?"

"Not right this moment," I said, surprised by the offer.

Josephine fondled the bottleneck a moment then pushed the bottle back into the drawer with a clatter.

"We could have dinner later this week," said Josephine. "And get to know each other."

"Could we sort out the money first," I said, embarrassed to hark on about this but I had many years of experience knowing how life worked; and the only way to get any respect was to demand as much money as possible. Josephine sighed, withdrew an envelope from her drawer and dangled it from her fingers.

"Money," she said. "Is that all you're after?"

I snatched the envelope from her and ripped it open.

"A thousand dollar loan," she explained. "And when you work you get five thousand, OK?"

I quickly began reckoning the sums.

"You tell no-one," she added with a yawn. "You pay no tax. Have a free holiday."

"What's this," I asked, on noting that the notes were drawn on the Bank of Hell, "Angel Dust?"

"People's Exchange Notes. They're pegged to the US dollar. The PENUS rate is seven point six to one."

"And how much a day does a hotel room here cost?" I asked, as I fondled the limp Bank of Hell notes. "I can tell by the look on your face that it's more than you're giving me."

Josephine picked up the phone and carefully stabbed at a button, making sure not to damage her long nails.

"You wait out there."

She waved me away.

I liked to think this was a victory, but there was doubt lingering in my mind. Still, I had money in my pocket and Heaven to explore. Although weary, it was far too early to go to bed. It would be best to find some sort of entertainment, get rat-arsed drunk and then collapse in a heap about midnight local time and wake about nine the next morning. Unfortunately, the only person I might be able to persuade to show me the sights was Sydney.

"I remember you now," said Sydney staring hard at me. "Cocky little bugger who was always saying characters should do the real thing instead of all this crap. Well, here we are doing the real thing: crap."

Before I could tell Sydney how thrilled I was to be there, how exciting this project was going to be, and all the other time-honoured self-deceptions one told oneself about crappy

15

productions, I heard a snarl and turned to see Josephine standing by the door.

"We got somewhere for you to stay," she said and thrust a business card into my hand. "Go find him and he will take you somewhere. Very cheap."

I did not know whether to thank her or not, so walked on down the corridor where I found an office full of brick-sized portable phones on charge (a cheap job-lot from the nineteen-eighties), a mass of cables, and a couple of young men in white T-shirts, trainers, and jeans, the standard uniform. I nodded to them. "Tang Kwok Wai?" I asked and was greeted with puzzled expressions.

I began to wonder if Heaven was going to be an infuriating experience and I would end up a gin-sodden old sod collapsed in a bar somewhere muttering about the inscrutability of the natives.

I felt a tap on my shoulder and turned to find myself staring over the head of a short, muscle-bound man with a round flat-nosed face and a few straggly whiskers. He had the look of Genghis Khan's lesser-known brother.

"Tang Kwok Wai," he said shaking my hand. "Some people call me Fizzy, as in Fizzy Tang. Get it?"

"Fizzy?" I said, "Tang? Ah, Fizzy Tang. As in non-alcoholic beverage."

"But with a touch of Tequila!"

I gave the appropriate grin. Then discovered the real reason why Fizzy got his name. Fizzy quickly barked out orders over his mobile to get his van out of the car park, take my luggage down to it, and then he hustled me along the corridor into the lifts while barking further angry noises over the phone. I kept recognising the name Stirling and asked what the famous director Lance Stirling was doing here.

"Giving me a hard time," explained Fizzy. "He won't pay my rates but I tell his guys mine are the cheapest and that I give the best service. And if he don't pay me, he won't pay no-one else. Ha!"

Fizzy seemed pleased with this idea.

"Fuck Ghosts eh?" said Fizzy, "They know nothing. Here we do things our way. You better learn that."

"Ghosts?"

"You have been in a long running series haven't you? Well when Directors die, they're allowed to come straight to Cosmic Casting. No need for actors and it keeps us characters in trim."

"I knew that," I said, not wishing to seem too green. But the rules of Cop Show Heaven were a blur to me. It was as if I had never been here before. Like reincarnation, I suppose, only the opposite – because this is where you come when you don't really exist.

I nodded as I climbed into the van, then looked for my seat belt, which was knotted and tangled and had not been used much.

"People got to like you here," said Fizzy, wrenching the wheel one way, then another, tooting and swerving, and turning round to yell obscenities at taxi-drivers.

I felt increasingly enlivened by this and enjoyed being driven at breakneck speed through the harbour tunnel and then out into the entwining roads. In the harbour, I could see the rusty dredgers and container barges darkly drifting before a line of shining hotels.

Fizzy took a sharp turn away into the main streets with their suspended signs, all unblinkingly lit, shabbily wired and scaffolded with bamboo. I craned my neck to see more. I could feel the lights flashing across my face and pictured how a movie would show this moment reflected in the windscreen.

"This is what you people like," announced Fizzy, "Cop Show Heaven as China Town; and you just gotta have a sexy Chinese girl."

"Works for me. Can't have a cop show without a night in China Town."

"And maybe you think you find Chinese girl?"

"Sounds good," I said. "Do we have to go straight back to the apartment or can I soak up a bit of the atmosphere first?"

"Atmosphere! Waah! Atmosphere you want?" said Fizzy. "The Dragon Lady get you all wrong. She say you only here for the money. But you want the drink and the girls too! Wah!"

"I'm here for everything I can get," I said. "Let's have a look over there."

Fizzy took a sudden turn down a narrow alley, then up into a multi-story car park where the van barely rounded each corner through a labyrinthine warren of parking spaces. Without a single pause for reflection, Fizzy slipped the van into a spot with barely room even for the sliding doors to open, and then hustled me down the concrete stairs.

"I show you Heaven," said Fizzy. "We have good time. Right?"

"Right!" I said emphatically.

"Hou!" said Fizzy, getting into Kung Fu movie mode, as he led me through the crowded streets where little old ladies in pyjamas called and waved handkerchiefs at me, saying their bar was cheap with nice girls. Fizzy brushed them aside.

"These places for tourists," he explained and then dragged me into a dark oaken imitation of a Welsh pub.

"Once featured in TV version of *How Green Was My Valley*," explained Fizzy, "But not any more."

Then he ordered two pints of Theakston's Old Peculier English strong ale and toasted me.

"Aaaaah," he said, wiping his mouth. "Where we go next, then?"

I had barely started to drink.

Fizzy led me out of the bar. I staggered under the effect of the beer as I tried to keep up. Fizzy had the right sort of stagger that took him through the crowds without mowing them down, but I could not do it. Every step had my feet trampling upon some poor old woman waddling with bags of oranges and melons. For a moment I lost Fizzy then caught up with him as he fronted up to a bouncer on the door of a garish bar called Coconut Candy. Before it, a young man vomited into the gutter and then rested against the street lamp lighting up a cigarette. Fizzy grabbed my arm and pushed me passed the bouncer.

"I'm with him," Fizzy told the bouncer, who was all neck, with twitchy eyes and a startling scar from the top of his head to his jawbone.

"Get in!" urged Fizzy, pushing me into the smoky throng. "Happy hour. Get two drinks for the price of one. Big bargain."

A jeer rose into the air as a young girl stood on the bar and emptied a bottle of Perrier water over her T-shirt.

"Wet T-shirt night," said Fizzy with a leer. "Usually I only come here with ghost. The bouncer won't let me in otherwise."

"I'm not a ghost, I'm a character!"

"A white character."

I looked around and found that most of the customers were young white boys in suits and ties.

Fizzy pushed four martinis into my hand and then manoeuvred through the crowd with four glasses of his own.

A group of young men wearing dinner jackets with Bermuda shorts climbed up onto the counter and launched into Land of Hope and Glory.

"Fakking twats," announced Fizzy, sinking two of his cocktails in rapid succession.

"Slow down," I said.

"Drink quick. Have more time to recover before driving."

The wet underpant contest was now underway. A DJ with thick dreadlocks chortled at the audacity of such a thing.

By now, I was pushing Fizzy forward as a contestant but he shied away only to suggest that I had a go instead. I could never refuse a challenge and immediately flexed my muscles, juggled three beer mugs, slipped my belt from my pants with one movement, unhitched a button, then another, as the audience hummed The Stripper. I moved like a pro and left Fizzy with his mouth hanging open.

*

I awoke to the noise of an electric jackhammer shaking the building. For a moment, I thought it was the hangover, but then decided that I did not have a hangover. Light streamed in through the curtains and I caught a glimpse of blue sky. Then I turned over and found my arm around a snoring naked Chinaman. This did not surprise me one little bit. I vaguely recalled dying just the other day and so it seemed to make an enormous amount of sense to find myself like this.

I looked at my watch, it was breakfast time and I was hungry. Then more information flooded back as the blood began to pump. I studied Fizzy for a moment and thought he at least had a good body but was I sharing a bed with him or was I just in the same bed?

I ran my hand over Fizzy's back and leaned over to blow into his ear.

"Good morning," I said.

I had never seen someone move so fast. I put it down to Fizzy's martial arts training. He did a back flip somersault over the back of the bed settee and landed with a thud on the floor.

"What?" said Fizzy.

I got up on my knees to watch Fizzy gathering his wits and holding his head.

"Don't worry," I said. "I understand."

"Understand?" said Fizzy, scratching his head then reaching for his underpants.

"You were drunk, I know …"

"Drunk?" said Fizzy, as he hopped about trying to get his leg into his trousers.

The adjoining door swung open and a sleepy-eyed woman with straggly blonde hair and a short red silk dressing-gown entered.

"Well here's an interesting development," said the woman as she ripped open the curtains and flooded the room with light.

I stretched to see out of the window. I could see more shabby buildings with rusting air-conditioners, windows full of dangling green flowerless orchids, and sudden bright red flashes of straggly azaleas poking out between washing lines of grey underpants.

Somewhere out there, dogs were barking and a building-site pile-driver was rhythmically shaking everything within a square mile. I felt a little thrill course through me and then fought to keep it hidden beneath the sheet as this blonde bent down to take a closer look at me.

"And who are you?" she asked, both of her breasts hanging out of her loose gown.

"How do you do," I said, offering my hand.

She glared at Fizzy.

"I thought we agreed," she said, "that you do not have a key."

"I found spare one and it so late I don't think you want me to knock."

"Hmm!"

She began picking my clothes up from the floor.

"I'll take those shall I?" I said, holding out my hand and hoping she would not drop all the money from my pocket. She dumped the clothes on top of me.

"I'll get dressed shall I?" I said, wondering how open-minded these people were or whether I should try to drape the sheet about myself.

Fizzy began to fold up the sofa bed and move it out of everyone's way.

"It may not have dawned upon you," she said. "The reason why you no longer live here is that I would all too often find you collapsed in a heap of vomit with some old drinking pal."

"At least I came home every night!" said Fizzy. "You should be grateful. A husband who comes home every night is considered a homosexual in my culture."

I tucked my shirt in and stared out of the window. It was a beautiful day, I thought, and could feel the humidity rising like a comforting steam bath. Suddenly the air chilled as the woman hit the switch of the air-conditioner and continued her assault on Fizzy.

"Some cultures," she said, "Deserve to be wiped out by imperialist powers."

"Haa, my wife," said Fizzy.

"Ex-wife," corrected his ex-wife.

"She's such a liberal. She eats no meat. No fish. No wonder she's so bad-tempered. I should take her out and show her some real food. This is Heaven. Food here is Life."

"Live," she sardonically corrected.

I noticed she had a gold chain around her ankle, which was a sure sign of tacky taste, sado-masochistic ambitions, or a penchant for clothing tighter and shorter than one's age group normally allowed. She also had little blue flowers tattooed on her toes, which was a sign of having spent a drug-crazed week amongst some hill tribe.

"Does this mean we're having breakfast?" I enquired hopefully.

His ex-wife said nothing but turned and left Fizzy to pick his teeth. He then mentioned that he knew a place that served very soothing noodles.

"Soothing noodles?"

"Oh yes," said Fizzy. "Good for the chest and the throat. Too much hot air. So we need some soothing soup. It's good."

I was not allowed to linger but was herded out of the room into the lift that stank of fish and garlic and, something else ... wet dog. The humidity outside was exactly like that of the sauna room at a gym and even before I had managed to walk out onto the street I began to feel in dire need of a shower.

21

Fizzy escorted me through the market towards a small noodle-shop. There a bald-headed jolly-faced man, with his vest rolled up to show off his belly, ladled out noodles from a big simmering cauldron of scummy broth.

Fizzy added his own lumps of meat and pickles from an array of tin cans standing on the counter and flipped a couple of five PENs coins over to the man who shoved them onto a naked pile behind him with a grunt.

He sat at a rickety table on the pavement and pulled a couple of chopsticks from a rusty tin full of disinfectant. The cook brought a slopping pot of tea and poured a thick green wad of leaves into a couple of tiny cups. Fizzy emptied his teacup over his chopsticks, wiped them clean on his arm then poured himself more tea.

"Eat!" he said. "Eat!"

I went through the same ritual, thinking this was perhaps the safest thing to do, and then began to tuck into the noodles.

"Soothing," I said to Fizzy who then grunted his approval.

"Good," said Fizzy, slurping at the bowl. "Japanese style. They slurp and burp. Good manners. Barbaric. They play golf, get drunk, and beat their wives. And drown Chinese patriots."

"What?"

"Never trust the Japanese. They're the ones who put the money up for Cop Show Heaven."

"Ah," I said. For it seemed apt that a haven for defunct fictional characters should be a Japanese-financed venture. A mangy cat staggered out from under a vegetable stall and climbed into the weighing scales where it appeared to die. This did not faze the fat little stallholder in her black trousers. She continued to serve and gossip with unique hand movements. Whenever she made a scandalous point to her customers, she dropped her wrist like some mincing theatrical.

When I regained interest in Fizzy, I found him talking about his wife, Alice.

"She's a hippy," said Fizzy with a belch as he finished off his bowl and lit up a cigarette. "A vegetarian in a land that eats anything with its back to the sun. And I think this was a great disappointment to her."

"What was?"

"That we weren't all vegetarians. In fact, I don't think I know any vegetarians. I know a few people who go to the temples and all that stuff. But dead vegetarians?"

"So eating meat was the downfall of your relationship?"

"We were in this novel where she meets me. She thinks I am an endangered species, then the writer decide it more marketable if I am a Masai Warrior, Alice then must be a frumpy middle-aged schoolteacher. She meet me on holiday in Kenya. Well, the story died. I mean, how can I be a Masai Warrior? And they are so boring. They just jump up and down jangling necklaces. And Alice frumpy? I don't even know what that word is! Grumpy yes! Frumpy? What is that? The writer got in a complete mess. So we end up here and suddenly Alice see that I am Chinese and in Cop Show Heaven there a lot of us here, because Chinese got two thousand year of failed writers, so I am like everyone else. And we're just colourful background. That when rot set in."

"And now what?"

"I got to get to work," said Fizzy, standing.

"I've left my things at your wife's place," I said. "Is that OK? I mean, she did not seem too pleased to find me there."

Fizzy tossed me a key and grinned.

"She'll let you stay," said Fizzy. "Because I own the place. It might be hers, but I own it. She will let you stay."

As we walked towards the underground car-park, I took rapid account of my surroundings. There were the red cabs pushing their way through the old women with baskets of fresh greenery staggering up the steeply sloping cobbled street. There were writhing fish sliced in half, hearts still beating, on great slabs alongside massive blue thick-lipped garoupa heads. There were baskets full of wriggling frogs. There were cheap grey suits on skinny old men with cysts and runny skin cancers. There were mouldy red, white and blue plastic sheets over the stalls. There were tall strangers picking over the vegetables, peering into the collections of antique electronics, watches and cigarette lighters.

"Foreigners," said Fizzy. "Come here think they discover place for first time. But they discover nothing. They just see same old thing. They never understand. They never see what the story is."

"What is the story?"

"Revenge. One day, you strong and you make me grovel. Your family big. Mine small. But later, things change. Fate puts some luck my way. And then I am big and you small. Then I take my revenge."

I felt waves of disapproval coming my way as Fizzy suddenly plunged into thoughtful gloom.

"Cop Show Heaven," said Fizzy. "They shoot people. No-one know why, which side is who, or what it really about. One side shoot. The other shoot back. Who know, but maybe they come my way one day. That's the story in Cop Show Heaven."

CHAPTER TWO

Josephine the Dragon Lady saw me climbing from Fizzy's van and so held the lift door open. I looked greasy, rugged, and capable of spurting semen in prodigious amounts over great distances.

"I had a bad night," she purred. "My leg. It was so painful. I needed someone to come and rub it better. I thought of nothing but you."

"Your leg?" I said. "What's wrong with your leg?"

"Cancer. But that's of no importance to someone with a healthy body."

Well that's a turn-up, I thought, a dead woman dying and I am going to have to sleep with her out of sympathy.

The lift door opened and Josephine, wearing a tight pair of leggings showing that she wore no knickers, wedged herself in the door, ostensibly to hold it open, but also to provide as small a gap as possible for me to squeeze past.

"Mmmm," she purred. "You smell so manly."

"I just smell," I said. "I could do with a shower. I'm having problems with my accommodation at the moment."

"I'm sure your accommodation can be dealt with in a satisfactory manner," she said.

I grimaced, but still pursued her, passing a line of bandaged and bloodied hospital patients sitting on the sofas lining the walls.

"I'm a professional cop show character." I shut the door on the prying eyes of the extras on call and sat upon Josephine's desk. "I'm sure there must be room for me in this production."

"It's not up to me," said Josephine. "I just give the director your photograph and your track record and he makes up his own mind."

"Then I should see the director."

"That's up to the producer."

"Then I should see him."

"That's up to the director."

"I take it nobody sees either of them?"

"Not unless they like your photograph and track record and everyone has already made up their mind."

I leaned forward, took her hand and pressed it to my lips. I muttered, "Obviously you are a glorified secretary and I should fuck the producer and probably the director instead."

"You don't fuck them, they fuck you," said Josephine.

"Just phone the director," I said, picking up her telephone and handing the receiver to her.

Josephine opened her desk drawer and pulled out a notepad, a pen, and then a folder.

"I am busy," she said.

I marched out of the office, making sure to slam the door.

A shiver of apprehension shot through me. I wondered whether my judgement was failing, but a PA turned up and gave the extras their call.

Scum of the earth though extras were, to be bullied and ignored in equal proportions, I followed them down the winding concrete stairs through a door into a darkened studio. There I saw a skinny young boy with thick glasses and the harassed look of the average director. Quickly the hospital set was strewn with walking-wounded, lights were shifted, blue filters pegged into place, wires gaffered up, highlights tweaked and the camera crew briefed as to where the main actor would end his speech.

"Should I be in this?" I asked boldly.

The director nervously looked up. I could see him thinking through the various possibilities that he had planned and could not for the life of him remember whether I had anything to do with them.

"Er ... er," stuttered the director, who then looked about for confirmation as to the reason for his confusion. The floor manager, a tri-lingual go-between who translated the sub-human grunts and half-coherent artistry of the director into the clear and concise, quickly conferred with him and cast a couple of glances my way. Then the two of them nodded their heads as if they really knew what was going on.

But in Cop Show Heaven it was very hard to know exactly what was supposed to be happening. The usual hope was that everyone knew his own job and timed it to coincide with everyone else's.

"No," said the director, improvising. "You are bad guy. You better see Second Unit."

"So I am in this then?"

26

"It depend. We have to see you in action."

"OK. Let's do it now."

I could see that the director was becoming even more confused. Somewhere in his notes, he must have sketched in that he needed someone like me but that was too far ahead of the schedule for him to think about right now.

"OK, OK!" said the director.

I breathed a sigh of relief.

"Go and see Fizzy Tang," said the director. "He fix it up."

The floor manager led me out of the studios towards an empty room further down the corridor.

"Wait here," he said, then left.

I looked about the black space, then peeked behind the blackout curtains at the window. Beyond were balconies of jungle vegetation and caged birds. There was a noise behind and I turned to find two gangsters in their dark suits, wide-brimmed hats and yellow silk ties.

Fizzy now appeared in the doorway behind the gangsters.

"This is Mr Ng and Mr Kwok," said Fizzy. "They are playing Triads."

Mr Ng and Mr Kwok gave a nod. I nodded back.

"Fucking skinny bastard!" said Mr Ng, while walking around me giving me a prod and a feel as if disappointed in not finding a plump enough duck for the wok.

Mr Kwok and Mr Ng went into a discussion with Fizzy. Then they disappeared again, leaving the room seemingly even emptier than it had been before.

Here I was willing to do my duty and show them what talents I could muster at ten a.m., in what was turning out to be a very long morning.

Finally, Kwok, Ng and Fizzy returned with various pieces of cotton padding which they began to wrap about me. For a moment I thought I was being turned into a mummy fit for a corpse in the hospital scene.

"It's getting extremely hot," I warned, the sweat dripping from the end of my nose.

Fizzy looked pleased with the result.

"I'm cooking from the inside out," I warned, sensing that I was turning bright red.

"Now you look big and strong," said Fizzy.

"It is quite possible that I shall pass out any second now," I said.

Mr Ng and Mr Kwok grunted their approval and suddenly flipped over backwards three times, yelled, "Hou!" and took the stance of the Stabbing Crane, one foot resting on the knee, the hands aloft in the shape of the neck of a big beaked bird. Then with a quick twist they span and in rapid succession flung their feet to within a half centimetre of my nose, before landing on the other side to take up the low prowling posture of The Tiger Prepared to Pounce.

I wiped my mouth and took a deep breath.

"So," I said, "what exactly do you want me to do?"

"You do something like that," said Fizzy. "Nothing fancy."

In my mind, I went through my repertoire of dance steps. None were quite as spectacular as the Kung Fu moves. Nevertheless, I could maybe do a spin, so I began to stretch and warm up.

Out of the corner of my eye, I could see that Fizzy was smiling. So far so good, I thought. Now for something that would, if not wow him, at least interest him.

I took first position, gracefully centred, steadied the breath, flung out the arms, raised myself on point and kicked the right leg out propelling myself with three revolutions towards Mr Ng and Mr Kwok. I stopped dead before them with hands upon my over-padded hips, the sweat streaking down my face. With them mesmerised at my performance, I grabbed both their noses, one hand for each nose, and pulled hard dragging them squealing to the floor. Now if that was not a classic finish, I did not know what was!

Fizzy laughed and gave a slow handclap. "Not bad," he said. "Not bad."

"It'd be better if I wasn't dressed up like fat boy Billy Bunter," I said, beginning to envision the role I was going to carve out for myself.

"No, that's good," said Fizzy. "You're big. You're dead. You have a gun. But Chinese Kung Fu beat you."

"You're still fighting the Boxer Rebellion, aren't you?"

"The period of this film is thirty years later," explained Fizzy. "1930s Shanghai."

"Thirties Shanghai!" I said, almost swooning at the thought, either that or the heat stroke. I imagined the clothes, the music, and the sense of doom hanging over a decadent outpost of the empire. Somerset Maugham and Noel Coward passed through my mind and I could feel the accent descending: the clipped vowels, the stiff stance, the arrogance and the pride that covered up the seediness and squalor ...

I began to tell Fizzy about my vision of Shanghai.

"A terribly Romantic period, don't you think?" I said, placing a hand on my hip and mincing across the room with one hand searching for inspiration. Suddenly I swung about and kicked backwards, causing Mr Ng and Mr Kwok, who had only just got back to their feet, to fall in unison upon the floor.

"Oh fuck!" I said as I clutched my leg and dropped onto one knee. "Oh Fuck!" I said trying to stretch it out and get rid of the sudden spasm. "Shit."

Fizzy came over, knelt and grabbed my leg, pulling it straight and pushed my toes upward to rid me of the cramp.

"Aaah!" I said, realising this was more than cramp. "Jesus!"

"You should get some ice on that," said Fizzy, giving me a hand up and a shoulder to hang onto.

Lightning bolts travelled up and down my leg, spine, and parts of my body that I no longer felt were part of me. Such injuries were common among extremely plump middle-aged men in gyms on cold Sunday mornings, but surely not among the forever young? It must be a leftover from the character profile I once shared with Sydney. To never be quite uniquely one's self is painful enough, but also to be grinned at by the likes of Ng and Kwok, as if I was such a Sydney-like suburban disaster, was more pain than I could stand and I passed out.

I revived a little and found myself stripped of the wadding and being carried into Josephine's office where she had a fridge full of ice packs for injured stunt men. Fizzy laid me on her desk and Josephine whipped off my trousers and applied the ice.

"You injure this before," growled Josephine, running her hand over the torn ligament, almost sending me through the roof. "You won't be much good for a while."

"I take it you're insured for this sort of mishap?" I said, looking on what I hoped would be one bright side of the matter. It quickly dissipated in the laughter of Fizzy and Josephine.

"If you someone," explained Fizzy, "We insure. But you not. You nobody."

*

"You're your own worst enemy," said Fizzy, helping me out of the lift and propping me up against the landing wall.

"Bollocks," I said, listening to the incessant sound of rattling bones that I could hear coming from the opposite apartment. "What the fuck is that?" I said.

Fizzy blinked a little, listened and seemed puzzled as to what I was talking about.

"That noise!"

"It's always noisy," said Fizzy.

"No! That particular noise. In there."

"Ah, that's Hell," he said, pleased with his powers of detection. "They're the neighbours."

Fizzy opened the door and helped me inside where he dropped me onto the sofa.

"OWW!" I said.

"Help yourself to the food," said Fizzy, "It's through there."

Then he turned to leave.

"Won't your wife mind?"

"You can pay her. I got to go. Busy man!"

"You can't just leave me …"

But Fizzy could.

I gritted my teeth from the pain in my leg. I sweated in the heat and sighed for the sheer futility of my existence. The Hounds of Hell howled on, the horns and ships hooters honked and tooted, and the electric drills removed, for maintenance purposes, the plaster from every single apartment in the block. They might as well have been removing the lining of my skull. To blot out the pain I tried to develop a positive attitude. I decided I would make a phone-call that evening. I would call my writer and tell him I would take any job. I did not care. I would even don a duck costume and appear in that animated feature I heard that he was up for. Nothing was going to be too lowly for me. That is, nothing would be, if I could walk onto the cosmic plane.

I tried to stand and grimaced as I clung to the back of the sofa. I hopped to the dining-table, a dark orange solid affair covered in books chockfull of alien characters and a tiny electronic egg featuring a digital picture of a indolent cigarette-smoking adolescent.

'Fuck,' I thought.

I was hungry. I picked up the plastic egg and puzzled over the Japanese name printed on the side. I dropped it as it beeped an alarm. Then the electronic gangster wilted, dropped its cleaver, belched its last smoky gasp, and keeled over onto its back. The death march buzzed out.

"Jesus!" I said.

I hobbled into the tiny kitchen, ransacked the drawers and fridge, and pulled out a plate of sesame seed coated octopus.

"Fuck!" I said as I returned to the table, sat down and tentatively, between spasms, tried a baby octopus. It was OK. Sort of worm-and-sesame-crunch really. So I ate the rest and then decided I would boil up an egg and noodles. I hobbled back to the kitchen and set a pot on the gas ring.

The front door rattled and opened. I froze, stealing myself to make a winning smile in order to disarm what I knew would be an angry woman. There was silence though, then a tentative little voice called out, "Mum?"

"Not exactly." I braced myself as I hobbled towards the kitchen door. After an explosion of thoughts, sensations, fears, clattering pans and water, not to mention the searing agonising pain of falling to the floor on my already over-damaged leg, I recovered sense and discovered that I had a fifteen-year-old schoolgirl kneeling on my chest.

"Don't move or your eye pops out," screamed the girl. I could barely breathe let alone move.

"Who are you?" said the girl.

I relaxed a little since it was obvious she was not going to kill me, merely blind me. My eyes could not help glancing up the short skirt to her white and pleasingly brief knickers.

"Don't even think about it," she said, reading my mind.

"I'm actually in agony here," I said. "Could we discuss this in a more comfortable manner?"

"I'm calling the police."

With one hand she flipped open her mobile and hit the automatic dial.

"You don't need to do that. Ask Fizzy Tang."

She hesitated a moment and the voice from the phone began to list in three languages, the services that were capable of being accessed from this number.

"Bugger!" she said as she clambered off and picked up the plastic egg. "Bugger! You let it die!"

"Excuse me," I shouted. "Could you give me a hand here. I think you've paralysed me from the neck down."

"Good! You deserve it. Do you know how long it took me to raise my virtual triad? It was ready for its first hit. Now it will never know the joys of dismembering another body."

"What?"

"My virtual pet! They're all the rage in Cop Show Heaven."

I managed to roll onto my side and drag myself out of the steaming water that now swilled about the kitchen floor. On reaching the living-room, I looked up and saw her seated at the table, pen in hand, taking notes from a schoolbook.

"I am actually in severe pain," I said.

She studied me as if I was some particularly unusual species of cockroach.

"Are you mummy's or daddy's?"

"I'm not quite sure what the question means, but your Fizzy Tang brought me here."

"Ah," she said. "You're here to cramp our style."

"I'm not sure what that means either."

"You're not very good with languages are you?"

"I speak English, but I don't know what you speak."

"Oh god, you're so bloody arrogant in your ignorance."

"I don't think you know me well enough to know quite how ignorant I am."

"Have you really hurt yourself?"

"Yes."

"Well you shouldn't have been lurking about the apartment like that. We have to be very careful you know. Illegals from Hell come here with their bad haircuts, break in, and chop people up just to get at their dried noodles. You're lucky I didn't have a chopper at hand myself."

"I suppose you could say I'm lucky."

"Too right you are. I'd be flushing you down the toilet bowl if I had one. No-one would notice. The drains stink enough as it is. And if you screamed ... well, we get a lot of that sort of stuff round here anyway. It's Cop Show Heaven culture."

I slowly flipped over onto my back and pulled myself up into a slump in the corner of the sofa. I winced at the pain and found those large blue eyes contained by a very neatly-packed school uniform kneeling beside me. The blue eyes and the jet-black hair made an extraordinary combination.

"Is there the possibility of food?" I asked, tapping into one thing that must surely be the source of some universal standard of human interaction.

"I can't chat with you all day," she said. "I must get my prep done otherwise I shall have to throw myself off a balcony and that will make a big mess."

I sat up and felt the pain subsiding a little.

"Look, erm, if I give you the money, could you order a pizza or something?"

"I'm trying to do my homework."

"When's your mother coming home?"

"Oh, God knows. She is so busy all the time I'm really very surprised she wants to leave, but I fancy California. Who wouldn't? Better than this place once Hell has taken over."

"Hell?" I said.

"Oh, you are new here! Cop Show Heaven was only rented from Hell you know? The place is full of people who either found Heaven boring or escaped from Hell. Which are you?"

"I don't know."

With that the girl forgot completely about her homework and disappeared into the kitchen. I sat listening to her whisking around the place, slamming cupboard doors, running taps, rinsing and shuffling cutlery. I became very weary. Long conversations without bursting into song, juggling, or some other form of physical showing-off always seemed to exhaust me. It was the improvisatory nature of conversation that did it. If I had a script, I could talk forever, but actually having to make it up without a writer; that was exhausting.

"If you're having a pizza," she shouted, "I'm having one too."

I lay back to relieve the pain of my leg. What a temptation and what a disaster, I thought. As my mind drifted, the clanging in the kitchen melted into the howls of the Hounds of Hell, the thudding pile driver, the ship's whistle, the car horns, the elevator doors opening, shutting, opening, shutting, and the drone of a TV set somewhere out there in the distance, in the desert, in the jungles, in the far away places of my dreams ...

My character was killed in a cop show and they took away my soul. So here I was languishing in pain amidst the noise of eternal damnation and temptation.

*

"You can't stay here," said Alice, shaking me. "You can see we don't have any room."

I roused, winced, and sniffed the air. I smelt pizza. Alice could also smell pizza and examined a note left on the table.

"Apparently there is a pizza in the kitchen that you can heat up in the microwave."

"Oh, good! Pizza. Pepperoni I hope. Where's ... the girl?"

"Lily? Oh, she'll be e-mailing people round at her friend's place. That's what they do nowadays, you know. They e-mail perfect strangers and send each other pornographic pictures."

Alice went into the kitchen and switched on the microwave. She was famished after a not entirely successful day rummaging around the tiny source bed of Cop Show Heaven's quotable people. It was a peculiarity of Cop Show Heaven that the most interesting characters never talked to the press – it didn't excite them – and the least interesting had nothing better to do. They were merely lonely. A pizza then would be just the thing to restore morale.

When she brought the pizza to the table, she found me slowly making my way over, bent like an old man.

"What's wrong with you?"

"My audition went wrong."

"Is anything broken?"

I shook my head and sat down at the table. Alice cut the steaming pizza with a pair of scissors.

"Fizzy's broken his fingers, his toes, his collar-bone four times, his leg, his wrist, and shattered his knee. In the end he was completely dismembered by a shark attack. And he's not even a stunt man!"

"Obviously not."

"He did the security on location when we first arrived. Someone offered him five thousand PENs to jump from a balcony onto a moving car. So he figured, what the hell, I don't exist. Mind, he wouldn't do it for five thousand PENs now. He's learnt that much."

I tucked into my share of the pizza and began to feel livelier.

"Look I'm sorry," I said. "I shouldn't be here but they said they would find me accommodation and Fizzy brought me to this place and I didn't realise it was where you lived."

"Yeah yeah yeah I know," said Alice.

"I won't be staying long."

"You'll be going tomorrow morning."

"I've to make a few phone-calls. I'll pay, don't worry. But give me a bit of leeway here."

Alice swallowed the last piece of pizza and took the plate through to the kitchen.

"OK, but out by the weekend."

That sounded fair enough.

"I assume the girl was your daughter?"

"She's something, is that girl," said Alice, giving a sniff of her armpits and wafting a bit of air into her blouse. "She speaks three languages you know? I can barely manage the one. She even e-mails people in Dutch. How she picked up enough Dutch, I'll never know. She tells me it's English with a German accent and a bad cold. I guess she takes after her father with languages. He could always pick up stuff just by being there."

"Met him at university did you?"

"Fizzy? University? Hah! The man hasn't an abstract thought in his character profile. If he has, he's broken it so many times it makes no difference. Last story where I was with him had him conning me into carrying half a pound of crack cocaine through Thai customs. Got us both executed. Bastard! I think the producer wanted a more positive ending or something and so, in the waste bin, and here we are."

I watched Alice pass through the living-room to the hallway.

"I'm having a shower," she shouted. "Don't come in."

Somewhere in the building, another voice shouted and another answered. Everyone was shouting and I felt I was beginning to get the hang of the place. Nevertheless, I was planning my escape. I picked up the phone and dialled London. After a few rings, my writer answered.

"Any jobs?" I asked without any preliminaries.

"Who?"

"Me."

"Jesus, there's a time-lag on this line."

"There's been floods. It's affecting the telephone lines."

"I thought there was a drought?"

"That's what I mean. It's the dryness of the soil. It affects the telephone lines."

"Who are you?"

"I was thinking of coming back in a couple of weeks."

"I can't tell what you're saying!"

The door opened and Alice made an entrance in a little black dress. The fetish high heels, explosive cleavage and her long blonde hair made a potent combination.

"It's very Cop Show Heaven I know," she said. "But the place is full of tasteless old drunks and I like to give them something to leer at."

"Very nice," I said.

"They're opening yet another Pig Out Plaza so I've got to interview Lance Stirling. Why directors need to mess about opening burger joints is beyond my imagination.... Don't stay up."

With a waft of the door, Alice mingled her Giorgio perfume with the stench of fish, fat, garlic and soy sauce and was gone.

"I'll talk to you later then," I said to the phone and Alice at the same time.

My writer was not a stupid person. On the contrary, he was a very bright person who had parleyed his unpromising acting career into a very lucrative career as a script writer.

"Hang on," he shouted. "Who are you? I'm sure I know that voice!"

It was no good. I clicked the phone shut and sat motionless revelling in the painful throb of my leg. Self-pity had its upside; it made one aware of the seminal moments in one's back-story. Did I really want to rejoin the living?

I distracted myself with the TV. I flipped channels. All the newsreaders looked dressed for a cocktail party. I entertained a fantasy about society newsreaders who would pop into the studios to see if there was any nice news to read. If they found some, they would charitably allow it to be played on the TV, largely because only the incapacitated would be watching. What kindness, I thought.

I discovered a soap opera where the director had left the actors to find their own space, which they did without reference to anything the camera might need. Then the TV went onto what I could only describe as 'irritainment' programming hosted by announcers in designer clothes and heated deliveries. The toupee apparently, was the vice of minor middle-aged celebrities allowed to produce and present their own shows. But then in Heaven, I suppose, everyone has their own show.

Enough, I thought, this was going to depress me. I would have to go out and wield my influence even if it was severely painful and would leave me a vegetable in a hospital bed for the rest of my non-existence.

I hopped over to the door. Hopping was not good, I decided. I cast my eye about the room and spied seven umbrellas lined up in a corner. A large black one took my fancy. I gave the brolly a few thumps against the floor. It felt sturdy enough to double as a walking-stick.

I left the apartment, took the elevator to the street and joined the throng. I spotted a taxi.

"You are taking passengers?" I asked, noticing the malevolent eyes staring from the rear-view mirror.

"This is a taxi," said the driver, obviously rarely surprised by the stupidity of the general public.

I saw the spiky haircut of this man and felt that I knew him.

"Where you want go?" enquired the driver.

"Where's Lance Stirling at the moment?"

The cab lurched into action. Perhaps this was my fate. I had come all that way – about as far from Hollywood as an action hero could get – only to get the opportunity to bump into one of Hollywood's hottest dead action-directors. That seemed too much of a coincidence to be rationally dismissed.

The driver gave a grunt of disapproval as he wrestled the taxi through the traffic lights.

"Pretty soon," said the driver, "We all going to speak a different language."

"I guess so," I said, surprised to find myself arriving so soon.

I handed over the fare and a tip, and the driver, as a parting shot, said, "And you'll all burn in Hell."

"More than likely," I said.

I entered Pig Out Plaza and a handwritten sign informed me that the reception was upstairs. I climbed the winding staircase, entered the reception room, and picked up my complimentary glass of wine. This, I reasoned, would make the pain in my leg subside.

I tried to find a face I recognised. Kid Prat was looking small and bad skinned. The abnormally large head and doleful eyes seemed to be the only equipment this overdosed screen idol had. It was apparent that the scrawny drug-wasted look was in demand. A few more pulled ligaments and a car accident might do the trick, I thought.

I was beginning to feel at home. There was Lance Stirling, looking increasingly like Colonel Saunders. Lance made films about truck-drivers racing across the US and blowing up vast amounts of real estate. Sometimes a monkey had more lines than the movie-star.

A couple of nearby journalists were putting away their notebooks as if finishing an interview so I pushed forward and offered my hand.

"What's your paper first?" said Stirling, pulling out a list from my pocket.

"Character, actually," I said.

Immediately Stirling turned his back and walked away with a couple of bodyguards trailing behind. Bastard, I thought.

"What you should have said was *fan*," whispered a bodyguard, giving me a consoling pat on the back. "Don't try to push your publicity stills onto him."

"I wasn't intending to," I said.

For a moment, I felt a rank amateur. I was normally so professional, but here I was being lectured in how to make a less than desperate approach. Perhaps I was oozing that smell of desperation that some figments of the imagination had. I had injured more than my leg in that accident! No, I had to stop thinking that way. I was THE MAN! I was the product of talent.

I was the dream. I was going places. I was not to be stopped. I was ... an unresolved conflict that still had lots of fictional mileage!

I looked across the room and saw Alice. She and Stirling were laughing and appeared to be flirting with each other.

"Alice, darling!" I said moving in on her, prodding the bodyguards out of the way with my umbrella.

"This is another unexpected guest," said Alice introducing me to Stirling, "You know how it is in Cop Show Heaven. People breeze in and out and you always have someone on the sofa-bed that you can't seem to get rid of."

"He's a character in search of an actor," said Stirling, his white hair showing distinct signs of a blue rinse. I shuddered.

"If you're casting for anything, who do I call?" I asked.

"Don't know. Depends who I'm working for. Right this moment I've a restaurant to open. That is I would have if the rain here hadn't collapsed the ceiling."

"And they haven't got a liquor license yet," said Alice.

"Nobody can get any license in this goddam place."

"What's the connection between you two?" I asked.

"Her writer wrote a script for me," said Stirling. "Used to be fine writer until he started trying to write something decent. Happens to them all. They have a couple of commissions and then start trying to write Shakespeare. I think he's teaching creative writing now, isn't he?"

"Yes," said Alice. "He's not writing much."

"He should never have learnt how to spell. Now, if you'll excuse me, I've got to put the face about. Only way to get the license sorted."

Stirling's bodyguards gave snarls as they passed behind.

"Aren't you supposed to be convalescing or something?" said Alice as she grabbed another glass of champagne cocktail from a passing silver tray and downed it in one gulp, shuddered slightly, and dropped the empty glass on a tray passing in the opposite direction. Then she pushed her way through the crowd towards the door.

I hesitated to follow her, but not for long, because I am a dramatic character. Mere mortals would probably just get drunk and leer down some nearby cleavage.

On the landing stairs, I rested before attempting to descend. I could not help noticing that they were a director's fantasy. None would ever resist the shot up the centre of the spiral where the murderer leans over the banister and the light from the chandelier glints on the axe-head.

Alice was below me and seemed to be in a heated conversation with a long-haired guy.

"There is no more to be said," said Alice.

"I swear that Lily is lying," said the man. "She is telling you things that are not true."

"Why would she do that, Padget?"

"She doesn't like me!"

I felt this was an opportune moment to make an approach.

"Let's go," said Alice, grabbing me by the arm and marching out onto the street. As we stepped out of the air-conditioning zone, the air flopped onto me like a hot flannel. Alice took me down the steps beside the old building and managed to have me gasping for breath at the first ten.

"Who was that?" I asked finally.

"Water under the bridge," said Alice, directing me down a steep crowded street strewn with plastic coffee-stirrers.

"The Street of Shame," said Alice. "Where the non-politically correct characters used to congregate in the eighties. Everything was more fun then."

Alice gave a deep sigh and pulled me into the stark neon lit interior of The Morgue, with its gleaming air-conditioning ducts and flickering TV sets. She propped herself up on a barstool and with little more than a gesture had Champagne cocktails ready. I secured a stool and rested my leg.

"I hate this place," said Alice, slipping another Champagne cocktail down her throat.

There was something burnt-out about her, I thought. Her looks were those of a once beautiful blonde, no, on closer inspection, beautiful golden blonde, with naturally golden skin and perfect blue eyes and white teeth. However, the thin mouth had always been there with its hint of clenched muscle. A nervy, vulnerable girl, back-packing about the world, sunning on hippie beaches, smoking joints, dropping acid, wearing flares. And always vulnerable, easily wounded, and seemingly hard as nails.

Alcohol and pheromones must be the true cause of the erotic fantasising that I indulged in. Then I put my finger on it; she was the femme fatale that any cop would protect and thus seal their own doom. Now that made sense.

"So you're planning on re-incarnation?" I said, by way of steering the conversation in the direction of my ulterior motivation.

"In Cop Show Heaven, if you have connections in Hollywood, you're allowed to go back."

"Ah!"

I was beginning to feel the urge to get on the disco floor and do some serious strutting. Unfortunately, the leg was sending paralysing shrieks of agony up and down my spinal column. I watched the little black square of dance floor fill with young things wearing cobwebs over slithers of liquorice panties. A strobe light struck up and mirrors all round the room lit with blurred shapes of writhing women. As they moved, I glanced at the door and saw Sydney and a young girl, half his size both by length and breadth, surveying the scene.

"Hi there," shouted Sydney over the heads of the crowd. "We're on the trawl for like minds."

"Well you found me instead," I said, a little uncertain as to how I should greet this man. "This is Sydney Poland, character extraordinaire," I explained to Alice who gave a thin-lipped smile. "He's my alter-ego."

"This is too young for me!" complained Sydney, watching the youth of Heaven bouncing beneath the strobe lights. The girl Sydney was with nodded and held her ears. She was about the same age if not younger than most of those on the dance floor. Sydney finally introduced her as his wife.

"I think you're right," said Alice. "It's too young for me."

"Come on," said Sydney, "I crave unbroken English conversation."

"Come where?"

"Back to my place."

I did not like the sound of that. Me and Sydney were like Matter and Anti-Matter, if we get too close to each other we destroy ourselves and leave nothing but hot air in our wake.

"Look," said Sydney. "I'm a messenger. That's my function. I'm a messenger from God."

"Oh yeah?"

"That's right. I'm like a Blues Brother."

"And what's the message?"

"Follow me. We must talk."

"We are talking."

"No. I go, we must talk. And then in comes another character who we cannot talk in front of. And so we don't. And then as they leave, having chattered about some minor character, I whisper that I haven't the time and that it is crucial that we get together in private because something important needs to be said."

"Oh, I see. We must talk."

"Exactly. We must talk."

"What are you going on about?" asked Alice.

"I'm sorry, we can't talk here."

"What?"

"We have to go with Sydney because he has something important to say."

"Such as?"

"We can't talk here."

"Why not?"

"It's too loud."

"And," added Sydney, "We have to go back to my place so that you can see what sort of person I am in a private setting. It's a character thing. I'm trying to broaden my appeal by showing a more domestic side."

"What the fuck?" said Alice. "Oh, for God's sake ..."

"That's right," said Sydney. "I'm a messenger."

Alice resigned herself to the prospect of meeting a more fully rounded Sydney and we all followed him and his wife to a taxi. Sydney's wife did the honours and gave the driver all the directions. A fierce debate over the quickest route took place, then on arriving five minutes later a fiercer argument over the amount of money supposedly on the meter. As far as I could see, there was no room for manoeuvre. It was there in black and white, or at least glowing green. But Alice nudged me and whispered that nothing was sacred, everything could be haggled down to the nearest half cent. And the taxi-driver winked at me.

"Did you see that?" I nudged Alice. "He's trying to pick me up."

"No," said the taxi-driver, "I've just picked you up and now I've put you down."

"Ah," I said. "You speak English."

"No," said the taxi-driver. "I speak to you whatever language you think anyone speaks to you in."

"Why's that?"

"It's all part of the creative process."

This was a very strange thing for a taxi-driver to say and I wondered if I had drunk something containing a mickey or something. I blinked, screwed up my eyes, looked sideways, squinted again, but he did not suddenly disappear or turn into a large white rabbit called Harvey.

"Strange things happen," said the taxi-driver, "When you are in Cop Show Heaven."

Alice was tugging at my arm wondering to whom I was talking. I would have explained but the taxi had driven away so we now entered the drab doorway of an apartment block and squeezed into the air-conditionless elevator, stinking of incense, and cramped to the point that I felt sick by the time we reached the right floor.

Inside Sydney's apartment, sitting neatly on three small sofas, were nine people caterwauling along to a stretch TV. When the tune was finished an old crone grabbed the microphone and began to sing the next set of screen words.

Although the crone was singing her heart out, complete with the hand movements of a hula dancer, the others did not stop talking. This was Sydney's family in-law.

Amidst this cacophony, Sydney boomed theatrically about how excellent his brandy was.

"As you can see," said Sydney, "I'm outnumbered. One has to fit in or not as the case may be."

"I know the feeling exactly," said Alice, now knocking back the brandy in large gulps.

I declined the brandy.

"You said we had to talk?"

"In a minute!" said Sydney. "Don't be impatient."

"You have something very important to say to me."

"But first of all we must increase the level of suspense. After all, if you ever want to be in a popular work of fiction, you must have at least one hundred thousand words and how do you think

43

writers come up with that many? By constantly promising people they will get to the point and never doing so! Intrigue, ask important questions, and then keep them hanging on waiting for the answers and explanations."

"I hate it when they do that."

"I know, but everybody is taught this sort of stuff and so they've come to expect it."

Sydney suddenly became interested in the singing and grabbed the microphone from one of the Brothers-in-law.

"Get the English disk and let's have some real music," he demanded and the brother-in-law searched through the pile of laser disks.

Soon everyone bar Alice was singing. "We all go ... onna... soomer ho hi deih ..."

Alice looked on in horror.

"When did you get to know each other?" she asked, trying to be polite.

I explained our mutual history, how we were different versions of the same character, and Sydney chimed up how between the two of us we could corner the market in advertising gold watches on the English language channels.

"Some things are forever!" said Sydney.

Sydney rolled onto the floor with the kids bouncing on his stomach until the music changed to "You Are My Sunshine."

I grabbed the microphone.

"Sell that song boy!" yelled Sydney.

I sang a duet with a hairy chinned old woman.

"Oh God," muttered Alice, as she finished her brandy and began to weigh up the glass in her hand.

And there on the TV screen was God. Sydney nudged me and I noticed that everyone else was frozen in time. The story has stopped, I thought, so that God could speak to me through the karaoke machine.

"Yo!" said God.

He wore a gold chain with a rabbit's foot on the end. He waved it at me and I noticed the chunky bling bling jewellery on every one of his fingers. I counted seven fingers on each hand.

"Hey," he said. "Seven days in a week, right?"

"Oh yeah."

"Twenty four hours in a day."

"Yes?" I said, wondering where this was leading.

Then he ripped open his shirt and showed me the hairs on his chest.

"Twenty-four," he said. "Ha!"

"Why the odd number of days in the year then?"

"You gotta have the moon and the sun out of sync see? Otherwise, they just stir up the water until it spins."

"Oh, I see," I said, not seeing anything. "So what gives?"

"I just thought I had to make clear what was going on, that's all. I mean, this is Cop Show Heaven, right? So me and you gotta talk before the chase sequences start. I mean, nobody listens to anything after that!"

"Oh yeah."

"We could do it walking along the street so that there's some nice scenery to look at, or we do it in some funky way like this. Like some Crazy Show or something where guys burst into song, or dress in drag."

"Oh yeah," I said, hoping not to show too much interest in that. That'll be explained later, I think. It's too complicated right now.

"And you know, when God appears in most fiction he's always just plain unsatisfying! I mean, I can do anything I want. There are no limits, but they always limit me. And I always say things like, you just gotta go through with the process because then all will be revealed."

"You're not going to do that then?"

"Fuck no. You gotta get your act together, brother! That's what you was put in here for. You gotta get some personality about you. You is drifting something bad. Things just happen with you. You gotta make things happen, but not just anything. Good things."

"What are those?"

"Hell, don't give me none of that shit. Good is what makes you interesting, otherwise nobody is going to want to write about you. This is Cop Show Heaven. In here you gotta get some dimensions to your life. Work up a good back-story; show the kind side, the mean side, the selfish side, and the generous side. Show you is vulnerable, and yet strong. Yeah, that's a hero eh? Isn't that what you want? Otherwise you is just gonna be a minor character all your life like poor old Sydney."

"Why can't he pull his finger out as well?"

"He can. He know what to do. But he ain't done it yet even though I keep kicking his butt. But maybe he jes like me kicking him because then he know I exist. Huh? You don't give a fuck whether I exist or not do you?"

"I give a fuck that I'm hallucinating!"

"Ha! That's right, boy. Look, here the history lesson."

God reached inside his shirt and pulled out a scrap of paper that he unfurled, and then put on his reading glasses and ran his finger down the words.

"This here is the synopsis. You know what that is, boy?"

"I think so."

"Right. This is what the writer got on you. So this is insider knowledge. And I'm giving it to you cos I likes you, brother. I don't do none of this shit for nobody else."

"You're bullshitting aren't you?"

"Hell, sure I am. But I'm God. I gotta at least seem all merciful and benevolent. So listen up. Here's the word: A character in a popular cop show, Dan Symmonds, is written out of the series and finds himself lingering in Cop Show Heaven. Here he must try and discover some depth to his personality in order to inspire a writer to re-invent him.

"Cop Show Heaven came into existence because heaven rented part of hell to allow dead directors the pleasure of making movies – I mean, there ain't no conflict in heaven, so you can't do good movies in heaven. Right? Anyway, the Devil wants it back and is not allowing heaven to renew the lease … Now that's a long story! But it ain't your problem. That's mine. So, you just gotta get with the programme and get on with it … Now, where was I? Ah, yes: Lance Stirling, a dead director noted for making talking monkey movies, wants to make a serious flick about the handover and he casts Dan Symmonds – that's you – as the hero. Dan however, becomes embroiled with the family of one of the stuntmen, Fizzy Tang. Fizzy, seeing a future for Dan, wants him to seduce his ex-wife and take her away with him to the fabled land of Hollywood. He fears that if she does not go with Dan, she will forever have custody of his daughter, Lily. Dan however … Oh, you don't need to know all this shit …"

"Go on."

"No, I don't think I should do that. Otherwise you'll think it is all predestined."

"Isn't it?"

"You have choice."

"I'm a character out of a cop show, what choice do I have other than following the script?"

"You gotta behave as if you do have choice. If I give you the script, then how's that gonna look?"

"It's gonna ... going to look like I've learnt my part. That's what."

"But you ain't an actor. You is a character. There is a difference. The actor learns the part. You *is* the part. Right? Get it?"

"Oh."

"Jeremy Irons is an actor. And if you don't buck your ideas up, you're going end up being played by him!"

"That's not good, is it?"

"Too right, it's not good."

"I can look at the character profiles though?"

"Hmm, OK. Just for you: Dan Symmonds – cop show hero whose writer inexplicably decided to expose him as a cross-dresser and thus consigned him to oblivion."

"The Bastard!"

"Sydney Poland – Dan's alter ego, who once shared a character profile with him but was excised because of his less heroic stature. His relationship is far too complicated to appear in the synopsis, but he plays a significant if very hard to define role in the story."

"Doesn't he turn up later on?"

"Well, sort of. But I kind of like him here. Anyway, this is your story, not his. Er, Alice – Fizzy's awful, but sexually voracious wife. She drinks a lot, fucks about a bit, and harbours fantasies of being a journalist in a hard-hitting contemporary Hollywood movie."

"She does, does she?"

"Yeah, funny woman! Don't know what will become of her. Ah, Lily – A Eurasian sexpot, determined to lose her virginity at sixteen, but plagued by political ambitions and a social conscience."

I could swear that God winked at me then.

"Fizzy Tang – Whenever Fizzy appears in a movie he is always played by Jackie Chan. What he really wants to be is a director, instead of a stereotypical Kung Fu character spouting bad dialogue."

"He says some funny stuff. I like Fizzy."

"Everyone likes Fizzy, but why? Beats me. And I created him, as I create all things."

"I thought the writers did that?"

"I do the writers! I do their inspiration! I do all possible ideas!"

"Then why I'm only half-formed."

"That is, I get the ball rolling. After that you're on your own."

"That's a bit of a cop-out isn't it?"

"Look, smartarse, essentially you're too stupid to be able to get the full deal. Now where was I? Ah, Lance Stirling – a dead director, known for making movies with talking monkeys and lots of explosions. In Cop Show Heaven however, he wants to make something socially relevant, providing he can do it cheaply and he does not have to venture too far from his electro-massage lounger. And then there is Cherry – a reporter in a TV series who is covering the handover of Cop Show Heaven to Hell, while awaiting the writer to sober up and write the second series."

"Cherry? Wow, she was in that other show I appeared in."

"A brief appearance before the writer moved you into his other scripts."

"Yeah, we have a long history. Does that come out?"

"Well, I toyed with it as a piece of back story to be revealed later on, then thought, who needs it? You know what I mean, Brother? Who the fuck needs too many complications? And er, then there is Edward – Cherry's rival, writing for the press heavies. Dan finds stories for him just to annoy Cherry who is being rather sniffy since his character was axed."

"Edward, hmm. Another old friend."

"Your old writer is going through a really bad patch. Really bad. All his shows have been cancelled. I think he might be heading this way soon if he doesn't stop hitting the bottle."

"Then what hope is there for me?"

"Hey, there're other writers around. A whole generation watched the shows you were in, and now, they'll be working on their own careers and stealing ideas from wherever they can git them. Hang on, here's another: Padgett – a minor dissident poet who happens to suit the political prejudices of a writer and offers Alice an opportunity to be part of an interestingly mixed-race couple in a Home Box Office, made-for-TV movie. He believes the Devil is after him, but he is far too boring to attract much attention."

"And that's it, is it?"

"There's me of course: God – a mysterious disembodied presence who weeps over the loss of the territory but does nothing to help ... I like that bit. And of course, the Devil – the inspiration behind many stories."

"You forgot one."

"The taxi-driver – the fount of all wisdom."

"Yeah, that was the one."

"And you forgot one as well. The turtle."

"What does he represent?"

"Nothing at all."

"Hang on, and the Dragon Lady and er, Barry, and erm ..."

"Forget it. There's always someone just turns up. So, now you know where you are, what your task is, and some of the people you are going to have to hang around with. I hope you're not going to just hang around though. There's not much time. If you can't get your act together before the Devil destroys this place, then ..."

"It'll be bad for me will it?"

"Maybe. Maybe not. Ha, see? Free will. You don't even need to conform to the laws of physics."

"For godsake!" said Alice, grabbing the microphone from my hand. "I think I'm going to pee."

"You are my sunshine, my only sunshine..." sang the karaoke machine, with a video of a man in a white hat, strumming a guitar, on a horse. "You make me happeeee..."

"Well," I said to Sydney, "I'll be in touch. But I think we'd better be on our way."

"But we must talk!"

"Later."

I pushed Alice through the door.

"Thank god for that!" said Alice. "Any minute I thought you would burst into *Feelings!*"

Alice lightened up when we settled into the back of the taxi. Her hand quickly went inside my flies.

"*Jesus!*" I said, causing the taxi-driver to glance into his mirror. The two accusing eyes reflected back into mine. Something about the haircut almost made me lose my concentration, but not for long.

CHAPTER THREE

I lay naked upon a bed with a single cover sheet to keep the cold draft of the air-conditioner off, and beside me was a cool blonde. I examined her and she was not bad for her age. She awoke and smiled.

"That was a very strange evening," she said, stretching and yawning and humming to herself.

This was definitely a sign that she had not been laid for a while. However, that Padget character must have been giving her one to get so steamed up.

"Who was that funny little man and his awful family?" said Alice. "God they were gruesome. I tell you I lived with Fizzy's family when we first arrived. I mean, talk about primitives."

Alice went glum for a moment.

"What you need," I said, "is a large quantity of food."

I leapt from the bed and trotted off to the kitchen.

"And don't frighten Lily!" shouted Alice.

I quickly cranked up the microwave and defrosted a body bag of pig parts found in the recesses of the freezer, sliced up some bread, and then fried the resultant bacon slices, adding some tomatoes.

"Very nice," said Lily at the sight of me naked but for a red pinafore that I had taken off the door. "Pity you're having a fry up otherwise I would have caught the full kit before school."

"Good morning Lily," I said giving the bacon a flip.

"So you moved off the sofa," said Lily. "I guess this means I'm going to have to be nice to you."

"Not at all. You can be as thoroughly nasty to me as you like."

"Did you check the sell-by-date on that by they way? We've been vegetarian for years."

Lily left the kitchen and began to collect her things together for school.

"What is it?" said Alice, wafting into the living-room in her silk dressing gown, her hair combed, and her face made up. She sat at the table as I brought her breakfast.

Lily snapped closed her briefcase and pointed at my naked backside.

"This is not healthy," said Lily

"Is your relationship with your daughter a very healthy one?" I asked. "I mean, doesn't she have nightmares about your obvious flaunting of sexuality?"

With that, Lily was gone.

"You could have mentioned you were planning on leaving," said Alice, throwing her meal into the bin.

"I didn't know I was!" I said, rather upset that she should suddenly reject me like this.

Nevertheless, Alice slapped me round the face and tried to kick me, but I pushed her away.

"Christ, what am I supposed to do now? Fuck you?"

Immediately the phone started ringing.

I found the receiver stuffed down the back of the sofa and picked it up.

"Hello?" I barked.

"Get your pants on," said Fizzy, "I'm outside. Hurry up."

*

When I limped up to the van, Fizzy handed me a brown envelope. I feared this was a threatening letter but ripped it open nonetheless and found two tickets to the circus. I examined these and tried to work out what on earth I was supposed to do with them. Obviously as far as Fizzy was concerned I was supposed to know.

"Like fakking gold," explained Fizzy in his best Cockney. I climbed in and Fizzy started up the van. He drove slowly through the street markets and pedestrians until hitting the main road, where we joined the queues to the tunnel.

"I won't be here when the circus takes place," I said, trying to hand them back.

"I knew Alice would like you," said Fizzy.

"Where are we going?"

"Location recce," said Fizzy switching on the lights as he drove into the gloom of the tunnel. Beside us, in Mercedes and Toyotas, the workers of Cop Show Heaven slipped into line and picked up their phones to wile away the tedium of the drive.

"I buy you a ticket to Hollywood," said Fizzy. "I mean it, you know. You go with Alice. Then Lily stay with me. She doesn't like Alice going off with boyfriends. I mean, you wouldn't like

52

your mother doing that, would you? Only natural. So she stay with me. Half of the sky is held up by women. That's what I say. And that is the half I like and I want my daughter to do her fair share. And I want her to do it where I can help her, not out there somewhere, rewritten as some Valley Girl."

"What the fuck are you talking about?" I said, trying to get my ears around the twisted vowels that permeated Fizzy's excited outburst.

"Alice a very nice girl," continued Fizzy. "But she want everything to be absolutely perfect and if not, she think you should move on, not put up with it. Oblivion is not meant to be perfect. There are things you have to put up with."

"Nope, the tuning is still not spot on," I said thumping the side of my head.

"You like her, don't you?" said Fizzy, handing over a crumpled banknote to the white glove that stuck out of the payment booth for the tunnel. He then manoeuvred the van through the traffic to the turn-off to head up the highway.

"Do you," demanded Fizzy, who was beginning to get impatient with my responses, "love my wife?"

"What?" I said with a laugh. "She fucks everything in sight!"

"And this is a problem?" asked Fizzy.

"Well I suspect it was a problem for you."

"You don't know what is a problem for me," said Fizzy, giving a toot on his horn as a blue wooden truck cut across him. "Bloody angels," muttered Fizzy. "Forgotten which side of the road we drive on."

A double-decker bus swerved in front and slammed its brakes as it reached a bus-stop. I lurched forward and hung onto the seat-belt as Fizzy swore and wrestled with the steering to get round the bus.

"I mean it about Alice," said Fizzy. "If you get together with her, I'll pay the ferryman."

"That's very big of you," I said. "There isn't by any chance a dead child at the heart of this?"

"She told you about the abortion did she?"

"Fuck! Bingo!" I said, recalling a favourite plot device.

Fizzy almost ran off the side of the road.

"Sorry," I said. "I'm caught up in an old script. It's Groundhog Day for me. Day in day out, the same script comes up and I have to go along with it until I can figure a way out."

"I'm giving you a way out," said Fizzy. "A ticket to Hollywood."

"First class, I hope."

"I'll see what I can do," said Fizzy. "But you know, within reason. It's hard to be the part that a major star plays. And being stuck in gestation and procrastination, it's hard to know who's hot and who's not."

"And you think this will make your daughter come running to you?"

"She'll leave with her mother unless her mother's got a more interesting narrative without her. This would suit everyone."

Fizzy drove across the light-railway tracks. He took a sharp turn into the winding road through the container storage dumps littering the border area.

"I can see that environmental protection is not a big thing in Cop Show Heaven," I said, peering out at the towering piles of rusty containers and old car wrecks.

Fizzy stopped the van on a drive outside a collapsing mansion. The walls were plasterless, the roof was missing and there was an overgrown garden. Fizzy explained that fifty years before, a clan leader had held court there. In those days, there had been buffaloes in the fields, and the lichee trees had been harvested. Fizzy tooted the horn.

From the undergrowth ran a couple of shabby creatures that quickly leaped into the back of the van.

"Fuck," they both said and breathlessly looked up. They gave a second look at me.

Fizzy laughed.

"They probably think you're an Angel," said Fizzy. "Shake their hands and smile."

"I take it we're not going to see the director today?"

I held out my hand and smiled. The two things both grabbed it and shook it warmly and clammily. I could not help but notice that they stank, their faces were thick with grime, and their clothes were steaming wet.

"Lie down!" said Fizzy.

They ducked down, pulled a blanket over themselves and went limp as Fizzy backed up the van, quickly spun it round and drove it out onto the road.

"Just look like an Angel," Fizzy told me. "Easy, huh? If there's a police roadblock, smile, relax. Flash ID card."

"I don't have an ID!" I said, alarmed.

"Do you have a passport?" asked Fizzy.

"I left that in the flat."

"You're supposed to carry ID all times!"

"Who says?"

"God says!"

Fizzy swore and then smiled.

"Maybe they won't stop us. You just look and smile. They never stop Angel. What would Angel be doing with devils in the back of his van anyway?"

"Devils?"

I glanced back at the two corpses lying under the blanket.

"These guys are hoping there'll be an amnesty after the takeover."

I craned my neck to see the bottleneck ahead of us. Half the road was blocked with traffic cones, and a squad of police with clipboards and phones in their hand were slowing the traffic.

"Oh Christ," I said. "I can see I'm going to end up staying here an eternity."

"Yeah, Lily phone me and say not to worry since you were disappearing at the weekend. She's so sweet. I love that girl. She think her mother and me made for each other and nothing tear us apart. She hasn't tried stick a knife in you has she?"

I was not listening. I was sinking down lower in my seat as the traffic slowly made its way through the roadblock. My mind kept filling with images of Development Hell full of cockroaches, grizzle-chinned psychotic guards, and no toilet facilities.

"Sit up," said Fizzy. "You're our big white hope. They pull over the vans see? But with you in the van ... Brilliant disguise eh?"

"Couldn't you have picked them up in a car instead?"

"You try hiding them in the back of a car. Three men in a car and what's that mean?"

"I don't know what that means."

"It means they are criminals. Don't you know nothing? You never see three men in a car unless they going to rob a bank. That's the way it is in Cop Show Heaven."

Fizzy drove slowly through the cordon with the police staring in through the side windows. I smiled as we slowed and then one of the policemen, all white motorcycle helmet, goggles, and adam's apple, slapped the roof of the van and waved us through.

"There," said Fizzy. "What I tell you?"

I twisted round and looked out the back towards the roadblock.

"Are they there every day?"

"Every day. Every month. They move about of course and they send back thousands but they also miss thousands. Cop Show Heaven's got a million illegals, probably more I'd say. No-one really knows. As long as they're not sleeping on the streets, nobody really cares."

I began to feel very indignant about being used in an illegal operation.

"Yeah," I said. "They're cheap extras for the producers."

"I'm getting lectured on morality by a guy who is fucking my wife!" said Fizzy. "And worse, not even having the decency to tell me he loves her!"

"I'm sorry," I said. "But you are trading off the misery of others!"

"That's right," said Fizzy. "And I'm offering you everything you ever want. No strings. You don't have to marry her. You can dump her when you get to where you want to be. Now that's what I call a bargain."

The two devils tentatively stuck their heads up from beneath the covering and then sat gawping through the windows at the lights and the people and the sweep of concrete roads twisting through the sky towards the tunnels.

Fizzy pointed out the sights to my passengers, then pulled the van over to the side of the road amid much screeching of brakes and hooting of horns.

"We're not supposed to stop here," he explained. "But it's near where you want to be."

He leaned across and opened the door.

I had been mesmerised by the passing traffic, harbour scenes, skyscrapers and neon lights ready for the celebrations. Suddenly I moved and leapt from the van.

"First step to getting written back into the story," said Fizzy, as he shut the door and pulled away.

I wandered about The Square and waited a while among the hordes of extras who gathered to meet friends, swap food in Tupperware boxes, sell old clothes and plot their rescue from a life of day-jobs as servants to ungrateful families from long out-of-print novels.

I checked my watch and time was flying by. Everything is a race against time in Cop Show Heaven. I had barely got up in the morning and it was already late afternoon. I had planned to do so much, and nothing had been done. I should have marched round to the studios and demanded a part. I should have got the names and addresses of other production companies, and started blitzing them with my résumé. However, if I was soon leaving, why should I do that? If I really was just in a period of rewriting and not really scrapped, then I should be hanging around the bars and joining other wet underpants contests. The only crime punished by oblivion is being boring, but none of this enthralled me. Renegotiating the contract and being written back into the next season did not enthral me either but it was an option that seemed more honourable than taking up Fizzy's strange offer; but that was whistling in the wind. It might never happen. I had no evidence that it would. All I had was Fizzy's offer!

I was hungry and had circled the colonnades several times, stopping once to join a group of tourists from Hell counting the bullet holes outside the members' entrance. Cop Show Heaven's buildings all tended to have their fair share of bullet holes, so it was a mystery why these should be any more interesting than any others but maybe these inspired some famous gangster movie.

A squat, pock-marked Filipina in a white smock handed me a thin and clammy sheet of paper. On the front was printed a big cross. Beneath was an address for some Apostolic Mission. A little band of Filipinas strummed outsized guitars and shook sets of maracas unrhythmically. They launched into a gargling dirge about the love of Jesus. I knew that this was a sign. I had to get out of the place before I found myself banging a tambourine, singing in tongues, and becoming part of a slide show shown to Melanesian tribesmen by Mormon missionaries.

I went off looking for a travel agent and hoped to find some other way out of here. I found them in a shopping complex and tried to haggle a cheap flight for the weekend. There were no cheap flights that weekend. It was a very busy weekend said Crystal, the young travel clerk.

However, I could, if I wanted to go really cheaply, take a ferry to Inspiration Point, have an overnight stop there, go to Lunch, where there was a four-hour stopover and then on to Development Hell, where I could make a connection with Air Oblivion to a suggestion made by the friend of the producer. It sounded a horrendous journey for such a hit and miss destination, and the cost of an overnight stop at the notoriously dangerous, or at least drunken, Inspiration Point seemed to make the whole thing more expensive. "No," said Crystal, all smiles and electrically processed crinkly black hair. "The flight is much cheaper."

I took a pen and paper and tried to work out the sums but got stuck on the question of whether Inspiration had an airport tax or not.

"This is a bargain flight!" exclaimed Crystal becoming confused by my insistence on working it out to the last penny. In the end I succumbed and came out of the shop feeling bamboozled. There was no doubt in my mind; the cycle of birth and rebirth was a bitch!

When I left the mall and pushed my way out into the thick sticky fume-laden air, I found a small demonstration carrying yellow banners. As they marched down the street, they shouted slogans through loudhailers. All the participants wore yellow jerseys and I noticed that one of them was Lily. I also noted that one of the guys carrying a banner was Padget. What did I care, though? I was leaving at the weekend and the peculiar dramatic triangles of this broken up family were of no concern to me. I would be camping at Inspiration Point, ready to leap, ready to trust to luck and maybe get written into an animated cartoon. It would be better than nothing, better than being embroiled in Fizzy's complicated strategy. I could see myself heading the way of Sydney and being perpetually irrelevant, perpetually out of fashion, perpetually incapable of capturing the imagination of

58

anyone. Nonetheless, I followed the chants and the rumbling drum.

Lily gave me a nudge and thrust a leaflet into my hand.

"It's in Chinese," I complained.

"Of course it is," said Lily. "Cop Show Heaven has one of the largest China Towns in detective fiction."

Lily strolled along with me, passing out more leaflets, even to a couple of policemen who were trailing the demonstration and passing on information via their phones to more police.

"Of course, half the demonstrators nowadays," said Lily, "are Secret Service Agents, and half the others are Special Branch. Some say even the blessed Martyr is a CIA inspired saboteur. It's all very jolly."

I did not know who she spoke of. That was her sub-plot and had nothing to do with me. So much of Cop Show Heaven is a mystery. The waking world is but a tip of this fictional mountain.

"Shouldn't you be in school?"

"Of course not. We finish early in the afternoon and then have terrible amounts of homework, but I can do all that tonight. This is more important."

"And Padget? What's he doing here?"

"Oh, he's a democrat. But he's a wimp. Not half as nice in the erotic fruit department as you are. You're not really leaving this weekend are you?"

"I've just bought the ticket."

"You rotter!"

"I thought you were trying to get rid of all rivals to your father, so that they could get back together again?"

"Who said that? Fizzy, no doubt. No, Padget was a bore."

"So you tried to castrate him?"

"I kicked him but that was only because he put his hand up my skirt."

"I can't imagine why."

"Exactly. A pervert no doubt. Here. Phone up your writer and see if they really need you in the land of mass entertainment."

Lily delved into her satchel and pulled out her mobile phone.

"You should catch him just as he sits down at his computer. Go on."

This impressed me. Here I was in a crowded street in Heaven trailing a Democracy demonstration with an illegally young

Eurasian on my arm and now phoning my writer in London. It seemed like I might be just the sort of politically aware, sexually rampant character to inhabit a prestige state of the nation mini-series. I imagined a dark brooding docu-drama about inner-city ennui, plotting terrorists and global corporate corruption punctuated by plenty of clenched buttocks, and arched backs.

"Doesn't that feel good?" said Lily as I began pressing the numbers. "I love all this communication! The only way they are going to stop us from being the most popular form of entertainment is to put Cop Show Heaven back into the communication stone age. Imagine the riots then! Take away their vote and no-one gives a damn but take away their mobiles …Ooo, now there is trouble."

"Hi there," I said when my writer answered. "Just checking about that meeting you were supposed to be arranging."

"Hello? Is this someone having a joke?"

"I've just got the ticket. I'll be staying at Inspiration Hotel, Development Hell."

"Who are you?"

I hung up. The time was not yet ripe. But he would come around to knowing me eventually.

"He said he was going to make me a star," I said.

Lily looked disappointed.

"They always say that," said Lily. "That's what my father tells me."

"Well my writer rarely has anything good to say about me so when he has I sit up and listen."

"They can make you a star here as well. All the Hollywood producers look to Cop Show Heaven for their inspiration. In short, you could be plagiarised by someone who knows the right people!"

I suddenly understood the plot. Plagiarism! I never imagined that I could be profitably plagiarised. I had assumed that I had to stay the imaginative creation of my writer, but no, with a few words in the right ear, I could be plagiarised by someone far more likely to get a script into production. That increased my options. There were, after all, much better writers out there; even the ones who plagiarised might do me that much better. I was getting desperate. All I had achieved so far was to become a crippled stuntman. No writer would touch me.

Lily pulled a spare yellow T-Shirt out of the satchel and proceeded to feed my head into it.

"This way you will at least serve some purpose in life. The Provisional Legislature across the border in Hell is an awful bunch of old fallen angels eking out some career boost by hanging on the coat-tails of their devilish paymasters."

Lily suddenly looked less certain and cast a glance towards the sound of the drums. She took to her heals and scattered all the leaflets to the wind. A policeman tooted his whistle and shouted, but he did not give chase for she was gone and somewhere the thudding drum doubled its beat. And all I had to show for the day was a yellow sweater and a stand-by ticket for Air Oblivion. This was not character development. This was merely filling in time.

*

When Alice found me at her apartment, she almost threw me out, but I presented her with the circus tickets. I thought it a cheap trick that no girl would go for, but to my horror, just as Fizzy had told me, the circus made Cop Show Heaven girls drool. I was thus in, and at least until after the circus, I was welcome to stay.

Although I liked Alice, there was this nagging doubt in my mind about whether or not being with her was the right thing. I would have hated anyone to think I was with them merely because of a promised ticket to Hollywood, but then it did not seem to worry her that she was only letting me stay because I had tickets to the circus. There was something very one-dimensional about Alice and this was no doubt the reason for her ending up here.

But who was I to talk? No sooner was I through the door than I began calling her "dear", and sitting on the sofa reading the morning's *Cop Show Post*. Together we were either a sitcom or being set up to be the Mr and Mrs Ordinary victim of a heinous crime.

My unease was not abated when I looked inside the papers and discovered pictures of the happy smiling faces of The Devil. He had shovels in all his hands and a horde of equally happy smiling little devils marching with him through a graveyard. They had been, or at least were supposed to have been, re-potting the ancestors, renewing their Bank of Hell credit cards, and providing themselves with a packed lunch. Devils everywhere were united by this one common practice.

I felt like one of the Ancestors myself. I now knew what the Provisional Legislature was and even could point to the map and show anyone interested where Development Hell was relative to Cop Show Heaven. Under the tutelage of Alice, I was even tut-tutting the Provisional Legislature's plans for making demonstrations of more than thirty people submit to police approval.

"Is this to provoke a public disturbance so that they know which key individuals they should arrest?" I said, getting the hang of the conspiracy theories that were whizzing about Alice's crowd at the Pig Out.

One of the things sitting uneasily in my mind was the kind of label I should attach to my newly acquired genre. Was I a liberal democrat because I tut-tutted these attacks on civil liberties, or was I a rabid old fascist because I thought the media was overdoing the panic in the streets scenario for crass commercial or sleazy self-serving racist motives? Was there not now a tinge of heavenly colonialism in my thought processes? Or was this a post-colonial liberal cosmopolitan outlook that denied nationalistic claims upon cities and proclaimed them as belonging to those that lived there and contributed to their culture? Should I applaud the localisation of the civil service on the one hand, but deplore the moves to make sin compulsory? Was this political thriller I coveted developing serious didactic pretensions and reducing its chances of popularity?

I think my writer was trying to open up a whole new spectrum of politically correct poses. Every serious thought I had ever had as *West End Central's* brilliant, young, but erratic detective constable had been about as relevant to universal mankind as the Muppets and cold, wet, miserable Sunday afternoons with all the shops closed. I was a parochial character that could not progress beyond the local market until more universally popular and no doubt sentimental traits had been grafted on. But I was journeying towards that great mythic goal via sitcom, now via agit-prop, and who knows where else I would roam before finding a new home in a popular Hollywood genre? I could sense that my writer was struggling.

My education in this New World was as rapid as I could make it. I went to all the meetings. I even listened to Padget holding forth at The Freedom Forum, about what was a real *local* story, and what was merely something imposed from outside. The local journos there complained that no "Parachutist", the term used for outsiders popping in for a couple of days to give commentary on the handover, ever dealt with the real stories of the region. Race, religion, and the struggle to free society from the control of political authorities, were the regional stories. The angels saw it all in terms of the end of peace on earth and good will to all men.

"Oh, the shallowness of the Heavenly media," I bewailed with more than a touch of glee. Before my opening up to deeper traits I would have merely slapped a few suspects around and then chased them around the block in a very fast car.

"My mind," I announced during many heart-to-hearts with Alice, "is being opened to everything! It is as if I have spent my life in a television box. My story now is going to be part of the real story. I am no longer an infant living in a fantasy world. I am developing dimensions. I am developing a Big Screen Persona!"

"Development Hell is right," I wrote in my diary. "I am a mass of contradictions and confusions and do not know which will be bear fruit! The good guy is no longer the handsomest; the bad guy no longer the man without a reasonable alibi. Nothing is black and white any more!"

Hell was buzzing with strange truths, with vitality, creativity, with an economic power and military build-up that must surely reshape the cosmos. Heaven was ignoring it, failing to engage with it effectively, seeing only commercial openings and thinking that saintliness was what it was all about. I, who had always been a reader, always been capable of studying my role, of learning the routines as quickly as they were invented, was overwhelmed by the sheer freshness of ideas. I was swept away by the manner in which the deepest underpinnings of goodness suddenly lost their meaning and retranslated into banalities, clichés full of sound but little substance. Oh, what a fool I had been! Oh, how two-dimensional had been my television character!

Alice however, seemed to be rebelling against this opportunity to develop. She complained how Hell never really defined anything. Like myself, she had been overwhelmed by the Devil's different insight into the world. She gave him credit for being so right about some things, for getting to the essence and cutting through all the bullshit. However, the acuteness of vision had merely led to a sterile, empty, and self-defeating undermining of the whole point and identity of the individual. The individual felt meaningless when words were a matter of convenience and convention. The individual was of no account when the onus of meaning was placed upon the listener. Then only those with power can say anything correct, for there are no definitions and thus no way of challenging through argument. There is only The Action Hero! He does, he wins, therefore he is right.

I extolled the virtues of mythic heroes and she dismissed them as having less depth than the average comic Cockney walk-on in a low sitcom.

There was a sign outside Hell's main ferry terminal that said in English, "Development is the only argument." This, so Alice explained, was but code for, "Trite is Right."

Despite our differences, Alice loved playing the knowledgeable local, taking me around Cop Show Heaven explaining everything to me. She took me to the Temple of Bochco to see the fortune-tellers. She took me up Sun Hill to view the Harbour. She took me through the Arthur Daley shopping malls, and then out to Colombo Island, not forgetting a few beach parties at the hippy enclave among the building-sites and power-station chimneys of Five O Island.

I warmed to Alice. My mixed feelings became tinged with more sympathy, more pity – though I would never use such a word. Alice's bustle, her knowledge, her prodigious capacity for alcohol and parties, and her obvious fascination for every single nuance of what was happening everywhere but within her own close relationships, overwhelmed my intellect. I wanted to fall in love, but couldn't.

She was an abstract sort of stimulation. She was a book of sexual technique. She was a fantasy that stripped down to the dark aftermath of brief frenzy, faded into yet another discussion on the mores and doings of that great faceless ocean and mountain of humanity: the middle-aged female character.

Not that I had any idea what I should be talking about instead. Simply to have someone there listening to my own tirades against Mr Bean – inexplicably popular even in Cop Show Heaven – was a welcome novelty in itself. Weeks went by before my sperm production dropped off to a mere dribble and I started wondering about life and whether having one's contract terminated was so bad after all.

So every day I would rise, get breakfast, lay the table, and read the newspaper making pointed comments upon the Devil's contributions to the British Conservative Party, as Alice roused herself sleepily, half hung over, half bewildered by my never seeming to feel sleep deprivation.

She would sit at the table, prop her head up and sip at strong black coffee as I dipped my soldiers, rattled my tea spoon and flashed her the outrageous front page photo of an Angel with the wind up his white gown showing off his bare buttocks. "That is just to take our mind off the forty devils they are sending to the garrison," I said, showing off my new serious turn of mind. "One can spot distraction tactics a mile off. Do your friends all feel manipulated?"

Alice groaned something about how *The Post* had its own pet Hellish Advisor, but this was not the time for discussing serious politics or anything else.

Lily grinned from ear to ear this morning, even though for most of the previous three weeks she had kept out of our way. I had taken this to be disapproval and waited for the moment when she would take some sharp implement and cut off my ears. But today she was laughing. She had found my diary, read it, and dropped it on the breakfast table to make her point.

Alice snatched it away and admonished her for being so obnoxious to have been rooting about our bedroom, where she was not welcome.

"The singing nuns will be writing you a letter," said Lily, "about what a shocking person I have become and they will be asking if there is any problem back at home."

"Bollocks," said Alice, borrowing one of my favourite words.

"Broken families and all that," said Lily, "are one of the most common causes of delinquent behaviour."

"And what delinquent behaviour have you been up to?"

"Oh, skipping school, that sort of stuff."

"As long as you don't skip your exams," said Alice, "I don't care."

Lily gave me a hopeless look as I tried desperately to hold fast to the image of father and homemaker that I hoped would keep a distance between the two of us. After all, one of the reasons why I was there was to put her off the idea of joining her mother in a remake of *Thelma and Louise*.

"I don't mind if she's read it," I said, taking the diary and placing it besides my cleared plate. "I merely write my actor's imaginary Oscar acceptance speeches in it."

"I should avoid beginning any speech with arse lickers, toadies and other forms of low life, no thanks to you here I am," said Lily. "I don't think many will appreciate it, no matter how true the sentiments."

"I write it down merely as an amusement," I said, trying to recall if there were any too revealing statements buried in the tiny scribble.

"You appear to be suffering from the second stages of culture shock," said Lily. "You are besotted with the new and disparaging of the old. All rash acts are justified as being part of your new self. Everything in your past is belittled and everything in your own culture trivialised. But don't worry. I'd say that disillusionment was just round the corner."

Lily slung her bag over her shoulder and marched out.

"What a bitch," said Alice.

"Perhaps though," I ventured a little nervously, but confident in having a very strong relationship with Alice, "she needs more of your time. You are always passing through. She does her own laundry. She gets her own food …"

"I pay for it all!" said Alice, getting annoyed. "For that matter I pay for you as well."

"No," I said, "I'm rent-free and I put in for the food."

"Who says you're rent-free?" said Alice pointing her finger.

"Fizzy says I'm rent-free. I don't pay him any rent and you certainly do not pay him any rent."

"That's because I'm his wife and half of this will be mine when we divorce and you are denying me rent!"

"Ok! I'll pay. What do you want?"

"I don't want anything. Just don't think no-one is paying that's all. Because, believe me, I'm paying!"

Alice left the room and went for a shower.

Thus, the honeymoon was over.

It was time to get the career back on track. But how could I find the time?

*

I met Sydney for sin in one of the large sin emporiums. It had become one of our little rituals. I took great delight in the clanging of the serving trolleys, the shouts of *Fuck Me, Fuck You*, and a myriad other calls from the devils that pushed them.

The crowds of squabbling families fascinated me with their sopping tea and screaming babies, picking horses and fighting for seats at the huge round tables crammed together in the massive halls. Sydney had introduced Cop Show Sin to me and made a point of passing on what evil he knew. I rapidly became a favourite with the devils and they loved it when I called them over: "Shit Head!" I would say. "What are these tentacle things?"

They would always reply with giggling and incomprehensible gibberish.

Between me and Sydney – who turned out to be something of a celebrity after appearing on Heaven's TV a few times – we would have all the steaming aluminium trolleys circling us and the devils chuckling at under-nourished characters tucking into the most unangelic concoctions of stewed head and beak. They would hoot with laughter when Sydney pulled a terrible face and ordered something particularly evil, slimy and disgusting. The two of us polished it off just the same.

Sydney was also a repository of the names of those to make contact with.

"Always the face to face contact counts," he said.

It had been on Sydney's advice that I bought a mobile phone and a paging device. He told me that things moved so fast, one could not afford to miss calls. That was the essence of the place. Things had to be done right that moment or you might never get to touch base with anyone ever again.

"But …" and this was the big question on my mind "…will I have to sleep with Dragon Lady Josephine?"

"She's got cancer you know," said Sydney.

"That's not exactly enticing is it?"

"Look upon it as a charitable act."

This was a satisfactory life for Sydney. Here he was unpressured and could take life as it came with the occasional exotic week in Sitcom Heaven to restore the batteries.

"It's not a bad afterlife," said Sydney, "being one of this crowd."

I felt I had met a man who in some sense had discovered the secret of life, or at least a fuzzy imaginary existence composed of bits of old rejected scripts.

"But will this lead to reincarnation?"

"Why would you ever want that?" asked Sydney. "Besides, I'm too old for that. Nobody writes characters like me any more. This is the only place where I can still find a role."

*

After Alice had finished her day's writing, I met her at The Pig Out for a drink. I expanded upon my theory of Heaven as a repository of unfashionable characters and half-baked plotlines.

"You're an arrogant bastard, aren't you!" she said.

Back in bed, she proved friendly enough but there was a crazy edge to her thrashings. She oozed and squirmed like a demented squid as she demanded more foreplay, more tongue, more finger, and went hysterical in orgasmic ferocity over sodomy.

"Cop show heroes," I told her, "never sit down!"

*

"Oh yes," said Fizzy, over the phone, as I lay in a luke-warm bath after Alice had departed to interview prostitutes for inclusion in a friend's book about the sex trade.

"She can be wild. You like wild though, don't you?"

"But I'm not sure she actually likes me anymore!" I said, suggesting that my mission was faltering and that soon I would be out of the door like that Padget fellow.

"Just slap her about a bit," said Fizzy.

I hung up, pondered that for a moment, and vowed that I would have to find something else to do beside play a part in Fizzy's little drama. I really had to get my career back on track. Time was running out. Time was always running out. A big time-bomb was ticking, because, that is what happens in Cop Show Heaven. The stakes are high, and being raised by the moment, and if the bomb goes off, there will be no ending and nobody would get to go home and return to the real world ...

Time was thus running out and so every day I just had to get onto Josephine, but not until after lunch.

But after a lunch with Sydney it was always time to pop along to The Pig Out. This would finish off the rest of the day and most of the next morning as well.

Again I would read my paper and watch the devil who cleaned for us twice a week doing all the housework.

I wondered if I had become the typical fallen angel with luncheons and clubs, and illicit nooky. I wondered that every day.

I would pop out and go for a cut and manicure at the barbers in The Norman Bates Hotel. I liked a close-cropped style that gave me the air of an evangelist. Afterwards I would go into St Peter's and buy myself a very expensive suit that I could not afford and was far too thick and hot to wear in lands bordering Hell. Nevertheless, the suits complemented the hair and next I had to have some new shoes ...

I realised that shopping and haircuts were taking up all my time.

I loved nothing more than to wallow in my own sense of personal crisis and it had to stop. There was a bomb ticking ... There had to be other people's crises in which to indulge. There had to be a new direction that could cast aside all the old pains that cluttered my soul. Time, after all, was running out! Something had to be done. I had to become less two-dimensional! The bomb was ticking!

Have I made myself clear? The bomb... ticking... ticking... and me, not entirely convinced at any level except the intellectual, that lunch was probably more important.

CHAPTER FOUR

I received a call on my mobile from the police. Lily had given them my number and they wanted me to come to the station to take her home.

Lily had been caught with a group of youngsters sawing through the cables holding up the new suspension bridge built between Cop Show Heaven and Hell. It was some sort of protest, I gathered.

In the taxi Lily breathlessly explained how the bridge had not been endangered in the least because *they*, the powers that be, could replace the links.

"Then why do it, if it was ineffective?"

"Because, stupid, by stopping its opening we can make it plain that acts of civil disobedience can be used to fight the authorities. We are demonstrating how one can fight back without violence!"

"I think if the bridge had collapsed then that would have been considered very violent."

"There was no chance of that," said Lily. "We only used a little hacksaw to make the symbolic statement."

"Oh right, it was just a threat of violence. But not actually violent. Just the threat of terrorism, but not the condoning of terrorism."

"That's right," said Lily.

"That's all bollocks isn't it?" I said. "I mean, you haven't a clue, have you?"

"You wouldn't understand. You don't understand what this is all about. You go into Hell and everyone can talk and you see the factories and the new roads and you think it is getting better. But then someone disappears. Then there are the executions."

"They won't be like that here. This is different."

"You wait. You'll wake up and think how you hate the devils. Right now you love them. But you cannot really love them until you know what is wrong and what has to change. That's what I call true patriotism."

"I don't love or hate any devils. I just don't see how your getting arrested is going to help anyone."

I did not like what I was saying. All I really wanted to say was the kind of thing people said in movies.

"Are we going to be telling mother?" I said when I got Lily indoors and watched her march off to slam the door to her room.

"And what of your father?"

Lily opened her door again as I waited for an answer.

"Only if there is any mention of this in the papers."

"And will there be?"

Lily gave a grin, held her telephone to her ear, and hit the auto-dial. She then proceeded to pace about the apartment trying to get through to news editors.

*

As I headed for my daily constitutional along Ancestral Road down towards Sydney's apartment block, Mr Ng and Mr Kwok picked me up in a flying swoop of screeching tyres, flapping car doors, and barked commands.

Neither Mr Ng nor Mr Kwok spoke much English but they were all smiles even with a couple of guns casually dropped over the back seat. I picked one up and it felt very real. Mr Ng – or maybe it was Mr Kwok – with a gesture told me to put it back.

"Mr Tang want talk."

They drove through the Harbour tunnel, then through Rock tunnel. Then through the potholed winding roads of the mountains through scruffy allotments farmed by metal-headed devils in black leather, and then drove through the scrap heaps and bamboo-scaffolding dumps, and then turned off the road into a clutter of huts and oil drums. A troop of devils lounging in a passing tree looked like a malevolent street gang itching to rip my throat out.

"Ah," said Fizzy, as I came out through the old barn doors of a studio near the Village of The Damned. Fizzy waved away Ng and Kwok, who dipped into the buffet for the extras. Behind Fizzy, dry ice curled into the muggy humidity, and the screams of background characters could be heard echoing about inside the corrugated iron walls.

Fizzy shook my hand and led me into a huddle.

"We've a bus-load of Cherubim on low rates so we're trying to avoid them getting into a fight with the Seraphim."

"You shooting something then?"

"Yeah, usual stuff. Angels come to Cop Show Heaven and want to shoot seedy, sweaty stuff; then they discover that

71

gambling's illegal and the seedy-looking extras are all fat and well-fed. So we've mocked up a vice den and bussed in a couple of hundred illegal no permit entries from the camps. Facking disaster waiting to happen. Keep thinking they'll all make a bolt for it."

"They're prisoners?"

"Nah, these are voluntarily going to go back to the clouds so they can come and go from the camps in the mean time. But you know, that don't mean shit! Any excuse for a riot. But to hell with them. Look, Lily's not to get into any more trouble. You understand?"

"I'm not her father. You should have a word with her."

"I did, but you can help. Hang around with her. Keep her away from those idiots she's mixing with because someone might want to make sure she gets into serious trouble."

"Who would want to do that?"

"Haven't you been reading the papers? You see what's going on in Heaven? They're shooting each other there."

"In Heaven?"

"Just do this favour for me. Keep an eye on her. Now get some make-up on. You've got a part to play!"

I entered the studio and mingled, while enthusiastically screaming and waving bank notes at a long-fingernailed dragon running a beetle-racing school.

The English director recognised me. "Just love that scar," he said, on seeing my face creeping into shot.

I was in a white safari suit and playing gin-sodden and crumpled. I had to throw a bet onto the back of one of the beetles and grin at the Dragon who turned out to be a very raddled-looking Josephine in a rubber suit.

"Nice work," said the director, his waist-length hair touching the tops of his khaki shorts.

It was a wrap and I had made all the difference and earned a fat wad of money.

"You saved my life," said the director. "Christ I had some guy … he's still here actually so I won't say much. But he was terrible. We came for the casting – but it was hard to find, and even harder to find it walking and talking and managing not to look at the camera and wave home to its mother. Know what I mean? We must have a drink. Since I'm out here, I thought I might do some documentary stuff on the handover. You know, video diary stuff for posterity."

He bustled off with a sandwich in one hand, cup of coffee in the other and his P.A. and Floor Manager consulting their running sheets.

I watched fascinated as the crew played back the day's takes. Even they were amazed that out of nothing more than a shed with a few cardboard backdrops they had conjured up a sleazy den of iniquity in an offshoot of Heaven.

"No-one will know it isn't Hell," murmured Josephine as she pointed this out to me and took hold of my arm. "Are you free for dinner?"

I smiled at Josephine and when in the taxi she placed my hand upon her crotch, I found a plump swelling of arousal. It had never crossed my mind that she could be a transvestite. I did not want to investigate further.

At The Pig Out we had a pleasant meal and chatted about Lance Stirling who was casting, as I had hoped. Though apparently Sydney was playing the part that I had originally been in line for.

"I thought it required a certain amount of athleticism," I said.

"They rewrote it."

"Why couldn't they rewrite it for me?"

"Sydney doesn't need all the padding."

"I see. No Kung Fu, just fat old man with a bloodshot nose would have been fine. You'll have to excuse me here, but I don't see him as being much of a challenge to your fine young Kung Fu experts. Won't they look rather like they're kicking to death the weak and infirm? Not exactly very honourable, mmm?"

"Sydney," she whispered huskily, "is a madman. Madman is almost as good as Blind Swordsman. Madman with fat dick in trousers. Very dangerous. He can almost make it talk."

The talking trouser department was a skill that had by-passed my otherwise impeccable knack for detecting movement in that area. Josephine whispered in tones of shock and horror that Sydney not only had a mistress, but that the mistress was carrying his child.

"When his women get wind of each other," she said, stabbing her fork in the air, "either they will kill each other, or they will kill Sydney. His balls will be fried."

73

In Porn Show Heaven slighted wives were sawing off their errant hubbies' dicks, feeding them to the dogs, or even in one case attaching them to a helium balloon and setting it freer than the husband ever imagined possible, so perhaps here frying is what happened.

"More likely they take his credit cards and bankrupt him," said Josephine, "But the whore has no family, so she is nothing. However, he is part of his wife's family and maybe they won't take it so lightly. Chop chop, haah! Her judge will be lenient. They want to stop social rot of one too many. It's a big problem now Hell is so open and their women so cheap."

Having one's alter ego castrated, though not without charm, did not make me think less of Sydney. I just hoped that our dual existence was not draining each other of the depth of character that might have offered us better opportunities.

Alice turned up, champagne in hand, having attended a seminar where local journalists announced that they were forming a society to promote a positive image of Cop Show Heaven.

"The Dragon Lady, right?" said Alice. "Pure show business. And this is a show bizzy meeting isn't it?"

"I've been doing an advert with her," I explained.

Josephine sighed. She could see that she was not going to get her leg rubbed that night so patted me on the shoulder and told me to phone and arrange a meeting. I gave her a hand squeeze as she left.

"You never told me she was a bloody man!" said Alice swigging back yet another champagne cocktail and ordering up a plate of pasta. "No hips and a padded crotch either means a colostomy bag or there's something else to hide."

"I can tell someone got right on your nerves today," I said.

Alice shook her head not in disagreement but in astonishment that she could be so pissed off about pompous men in suits defending political apathy.

"It is the guilt that one sees behind it all," explained Alice.

As Alice droned on about just when the devils would forget their promises of autonomy and throw us all into the fires, I thought of what Lily was doing presently, and whether it would involve Fizzy breaking my legs for letting her do it.

I excused myself, saying how I had to go to the loo. I walked out onto the landing and down the stairs to the foyer where I could see the computer terminals impressively tuned into news services and websites. Impatiently tapping away at one was a very dark suit enveloping a sweaty, red-faced man with a red-haired woman standing beside him. I recognised both from the notes our writer left in the script margins.

"Cherry fucking Halligan!" I said, and could not help but feel a strange sense of relief.

Cherry stared at me and the expression on her face told me that she did not think my presence a very welcome one.

"Cherry darling!" I said, kissing her on both cheeks just to turn her face the same colour as her hair. "And ..."

I looked at the man and could not recall his name.

"And ... Newspaper Correspondent Man."

"Edward," said Edward.

"Eddy," I said, shaking his hand. "Good to see you out here. You look like you've been well, hard at work."

"So," said Cherry, regaining her composure. "I didn't know you were here."

"Obviously not," I said. "How's Jake?"

"He's alright I suppose. I wouldn't know."

"Ah," I said, reading between the lines. "Well, never mind then. I guess anyone who would risk being on a murder charge rather than let his wife know he was having an affair was not going to prove to be a life long commitment."

I assumed the series where she and Edward were major characters had run its course and either killed them off or been axed entirely. The writer we held in common had turned to alcohol by now.

"Something like that," she said.

"Well I suppose you've come to interview everyone have you? You and six thousand others I understand."

"I don't think we will be allowed to, do you?" said Cherry. "We've been listening to that talk upstairs. A bunch of pompous old farts have been telling us that we can't do our jobs and report things like how the Devil will be riding into Heaven on a large black horse and that there will be much wailing and gnashing of teeth. The Devil, apparently, is just a good-hearted lad that nobody need fear."

"I suppose it's a bit late for the angels to start worrying about that, isn't it?" I said.

I felt hot breath on my neck and smelt the brandy and champagne fumes. Alice's blonde hair fell over my shoulders as she rested her chin on me. She glared at Cherry and Edward, both in black suits.

"A couple of friends from the character outlines," I explained.

Alice limply offered her hand to be shaken, which it was by Cherry and Edward in good, solid, firm British style. Alice managed a slight belch.

"Ah yes," she said. "You were the one asking all those questions."

"And getting stupid answers," said Cherry.

"Of course," said Alice. "I could have written for *The Times*, but they said they would rather send their own man here. A fucking *man!* Rather than use a mere local who knew intimately … I tell you, we know these guys. We know their background right? But they would rather pay some fucking little toad of a man to drop in here and hang about the fucking bar talking to us, and then write it all up and send it back."

"Well no wonder we get all the facts wrong," said Cherry, looking for an escape from this. "Excuse me. I must talk to that person at the far end over there."

As she moved, she parted the crowd before her. The noise dropped and all I could hear was the whispering noises of her thighs brushing against each other.

"That bitch is running away from me!" said Alice with a look of horror. "She thinks I am third rate doesn't she?"

Alice left the room heading in the direction of the ladies' room. I almost followed, worrying that I would have to fish her out of a cubicle covered in vomit, but then decided that Alice had managed to get into such a legless state on so many occasions without such a disaster that I should not worry too much.

"Had a bit too much has she?" said Edward, picking up my glass from the top of the computer. "First drunk I've seen since I've been here. Although there's a lot of near drunks, but she's the first stereotypically drunk."

"Drinking yourself sick isn't a big thing here."

"Of course the Cop Show Heaven lot are right," said Edward. "The story we're supposed to have is Cop Show Heaven reeling under the impact of tragic events. Haven't seen any yet but we have hopes."

Under normal circumstances I would have been preparing my sound bites and trying to fish up from the back of my mind a suitable atrocity to pass on. I liked to give good copy when I could. One episode I was in had me doing an *LA Confidential* sort of thing, getting in with the local press and getting high on the heroic reporting of my crime-busting activities. I should have realised then that my character had become ironic and that the writer no longer took popular television seriously.

Edward was most likely a similar victim of writerly hubris. I could imagine the drunken no-hoper now struggling to write *War and Peace* and neglecting the cop show episodes he paid his mortgage with.

"You might be able to help me though," said Edward. "I'm doing an end-of-creation piece and I've been looking for end-of-creation sort of things."

"There are a few angels making sandwiches rather than running multi-nationals nowadays."

"Oh yeah, I've done *The Good Times are Over, The Fat Cats are Fleeing* sort of stuff. What I want is real characters with real stories."

"Can't help you there. It's not really a Cop Show Heaven thing."

"Then I'm stuck. I mean, Political Correctness and Multi-Culturalism begin to look pretty silly when you've no existence in the real world. Is there an Atheist Heaven by the way?"

"I think they call it Hell."

"Ah yeah, it must be a bit of a bummer to find yourself before God who then proceeds to spend an eternity saying, 'I told you so, but would you listen?'"

I heard the faint groan of a woman and a pale-looking Alice beckoned that it was time for her to be taken home and put to bed. I said my goodbyes and exchanged cards. I would do my best to help him.

I mentioned this in the cab home but Alice did not hear me. She was fast asleep and was still fast asleep when I dropped her into the bed and stripped her. She stank of vomit, stale smoke and spilled drinks. The allure had gone out of our relationship.

Cherry on the other hand was as pristine and in control as ever. I could not help but see her in black latex bending a whip in her hand. Be gone evil thoughts, I thought and then checked in on Lily's room. There she was naked in the warm night laid out in perfect detail, oozing jasmine. I should have withdrawn from the room. However, I lingered and counted her pubic hairs.

I departed sweating and about as dangerously explosive as a man could get without his zip fastener flaying the paint off the wall. This was passion indeed. This was love.

I lay in bed beside Alice and sighed myself to sleep and nocturnal emissions.

*

The next morning Alice slept in. A glass of supposedly quick-acting Nuke failed to relieve her hangover and she for the first time felt her liver was failing. She would be dead by the afternoon we concluded, and the only cure was more Nuke and not to move or make sudden noises while hiding from the light of day.

I felt that I was betraying her when I phoned Edward and arranged for him to come and meet with Lily's friends. This would be another excuse for sticking with Lily, who seemed to have abandoned school altogether. "I'm ahead of the game anyway," she said, pointing out that being a fictional character makes a folly of education.

Lily and I met with Edward outside the courthouse and went for a stroll through the park. There Lily collected up more friends, the aim being to let Edward get to know them. The group was in its twenties and wanted to disassociate itself from the usual rent-a-crowd one saw on TV. It was a cultural pressure group, so the members informed Edward, since three played in one of the few heavy-metal bands, proudly informing Edward that they could play Hell off the stage.

"Uh huh," said Edward, wondering where all this was leading.

Die Nasty, as the rockers called themselves, immediately fell to arguing about what living the life meant for characters who had failed to appear in any published work before.

A plump little girl with four-inch thick soles on her shoes, squeaked on about religious freedom. She was apparently a Christian and was disgusted that there were no Christian schools in Cop Show Heaven. This was disputed by Mr Hung, a gruff middle-aged gentlemen with a leather handbag and a big chunky belt that I recognised as a hallmark of Hell.

Mr Hung thought poetry was the way forward because everyone in Cop Show Heaven read only comic books and that would not equip them to combat the philistine forces of Hell's iconoclastic nature. Lily had a go at him for still fighting the battles of The Fall.

I became desperate since I had organised Edward's meeting, hoping they could answer his questions. However, whatever Edward asked was ignored.

"I can see that you all have particular concerns and pursuits," said Edward. "But what do you feel about Hell's take-over?"

Die Nasty told him that the punk revivalists of Sitcom Heaven were pumping out obscene pirate versions of the Devil's Own Tune. "But they want to kill everyone where we want to fuck 'em!"

I pointed out to Edward that this group had recently been arrested for trying to saw the suspension bridge in half.

"It would have been beautiful," said Mr Hung.

Edward was getting excited but I could not get anyone to explain that statement. What I did get were the members of Die Nasty enacting the proceedings of God's Legislature, which usually debated everything with a fistfight. At that point, they threatened to go burn some tyres outside the Devil's News Agency.

I called it a day, thanked everyone for their time and persuaded Die Nasty to give Edward his tape-recorder back, which they did after singing one of Mr Hung's poems. Mr Hung apparently was Die Nasty's lyricist and currently working on a Rock Musical that they hoped to make into a film. It was going to be all about Cancelling The Show.

"There's going to be all these great chicks in little khaki shorts."

At that point they all wanted to know who in posterity would be the best person for them to contact because they thought my writer obviously needed a new project. I informed them that they had him wrong and ushered Edward away towards the nearest deli on Wayward Road.

Lily would have gone off with the band but I took her hand and she meekly followed on.

"I got a story," said Edward. "I really did."

"What sort of story," said Lily bitterly. "That we are all idiots?"

"The Paralysis of Protest brought on by the desire to be rid of the feeling that one is no longer bad anymore."

"That's not it!" said Lily.

"What is it?" said Edward. "That you're all too rich and fat to give a toss one way or another?"

"Stick with Paralysis of Protest," I advised Lily. "You're reasonably ahead of the game there."

"Most likely," said Edward, "that's why no-one in Cop Show Heaven ever recognises themselves in the world's press. It's just too difficult to find out what is really going on."

"We speak English!" said Lily.

"Of a sorts," muttered Edward with a smug little acknowledgement between me and him, which disgruntled Lily even more.

"That woman I saw you with last night …" said Edward while spooning the froth off his coffee into his mouth.

"Lily's mother," I hastened to say in case something unflattering was about to be said.

"Ah," said Edward. "Those blue eyes are quite extraordinary."

Lily blushed.

Edward got up to leave, gave me thanks, shook my hand and went on his way, flinching from the waft of heat that hit him on opening the door.

"I shouldn't get too depressed," I said to cheer up Lily.

For a moment we held hands and looked into each other's eyes.

Fuck, I thought, my writer must be applying for jobs on teen soaps.

Lily pulled her phone from her rucksack.

"I'm supposed to be meeting up with some school friends. We thought we might go to the cinema. Do you want to come?"

I shook my head. There were things of far more importance to do if I wished to re-establish my existence in the world of fiction.

*

Alice recovered from her hangover, returned to work, and ignored me for a while. She was determined to make the Devil's arrival a very good career move. She even talked of cracking some papers run by psychics trying to print tomorrow's news. Then if she was noticed, there was syndication. This would pave her way for that move to Hollywood.

With this new resolve she went off to try to get the best stories. Her idea of research was coffee, lunch, and drinks with various "insiders" who in theory would point her to the "real" story ahead of the pack. It was always a matter of bitterness to discover the pack creating its own story by consensus, often leaving her with what editors turned down as too parochial even though she assured them it was true.

Since Alice was on a quest to prove she was more than just a housewife, I could have a longer lunch break with Sydney. I asked him about his mistress and Sydney confessed that she was wonderful but he did not know what to do with her. He loved her and he loved his wife. He loved them both equally and felt that may be badly characterised women did not mind so long as they were treated equally.

"They can become sisters," said Sydney. "And there are plenty of cases in literature where sisters are the best of friends and share the love and devotion of their man."

"You're living in a fantasy world," I said and ate another spoonful of tofu in sugar and rosewater. "What will her brothers do?" I asked.

"They're men and she's just a girl. It won't come to anything like that. But I don't know what it will come to, because there's another girl as well."

I took a close look at this little grey-haired man.

"Fuck me Sydney! Actually, don't fuck me Sydney. But fuck me, you are the man with the chocolate dick, aren't you? I thought it was just an old wives' tale but no, you've a rod of fruit and nut."

"A man has to maintain his self respect somehow," he said. "Maybe if I was a great character, I would not be such a great lover. It is one of the few consolations of my old age."

"Don't give me that! You even got my role in the script!"

I began to feel sorry for myself. For here was an out-take from my own character profile, who, for all my undoubted lack of talent, was doing better than I was. Sydney cheered me up with some more news about Stirling's new film.

"Is it action adventure?" I asked hoping that I would fit the part of a James Bond type among the bikini-clad girls.

"Well I don't know," said Sydney. "I think old Stirling's gone a bit soft. He wants to do something sensitive."

"Sensitivity in a Stirling movie?"

"I know it's a big joke but he talked of it being his *Schindler's List.* I think the Cherubim riots at the detention centre have impressed him."

Sydney wished me luck and trotted off to meet up with the latest little demon.

"Give her one for me," I said.

The man with the chocolate dick was if anything uglier than most people could appreciate. I was morally bankrupt, an admirable quality for anyone in the entertainment business, but he was ugly.

*

Stirling was surprisingly accommodating when I arrived at his office. Before him on the table was an array of portable phones, bottles of brandy and boxes of cigars. He chomped a cigar as if it was a sausage and was a little surprised that I had been so quick off the mark; but when told that Sydney put me his way, Stirling grinned.

"Sydney," he said fondly. "That guy knows every brothel and karaoke hostess bar in Cop Show Heaven. But they're unhealthy. The girl might be OK but when you go into a room with a roll of toilet paper hanging from the ceiling, you need some kind of implantation to finish what you started."

"Sydney's speciality, I understand."

"In Porno Film Parlance, he is Iron Man …"

Stirling turned out to be a connoisseur of porno movies. Some of his most pleasant film-making experiences had been when he fell to turning out the cheap and dirty. Everyone with wide collars, pancho villa mustachios and Afros was getting laid by babes to the strains of a Hammond organ playing variations of 'Je t'aime' for forty minutes.

"If only somebody had written a young Sydney," said Stirling, "I could have made him a star. But he's fit only for speciality Bizarros. He'd have to fuck a chicken or something to recoup costs. Mind, Sydney's a guy I'd have faith in for that."

Since his death, Stirling had been delving into the undertow of Cop Show Heaven society, not only out of nostalgia for the innocence of his youth, but also as part of his research for the present movie. He wanted me – or anyone that he could get at short notice – to play a Brit in town.

"He comes across some pretty strong evidence of collusion between the Archangels and the Hounds of Hell," explained Stirling. "Do you know the Police Chief of Hades called them patriotic?"

Stirling explained the thesis of his film; that gangsters were being used to maintain "stability" by targeting troublemakers for the Devil.

I nodded and tried to imagine the scenario.

"All this stuff in Sitcom Heaven, all these gang killings and shoot-outs, they're all to do with the battle between Hades and Hell and the Sitcom police losing all authority."

"Aren't they the same place?"

"We haven't got the script fixed yet."

I nodded. I knew the score.

"But we got the money!" said Stirling cheerfully. "Which is all that counts!"

Stirling laughed cheerfully, poured himself a brandy, and gestured to an assistant to bring him some sheets of hotly faxed script.

"The writer's in Purgatory faxing the sheets off his computer. I'm not happy with it yet but I think he's getting there. We'll drive him insane in the process but we'll get what we need."

Stirling was on his feet and running energetically through one of the big moments that happened in the opening sequence. He was on a motorcycle: – That is, he swivelled his chair back to front and sat astride it. He was then blasting away two-handed, then leaping off and gesturing that this was where he was rolling across the road under the wheels of passing cars as the gangland boss caught in the back of his car lay bleeding. His henchmen were desperately trying to get across the road to kill the assassin. He whips off his helmet as he hits the gutter, revealing that he isn't a pointy-headed devil but a Brit. Then in the confusion, he blends into the cowering crowd of tourists, and the henchmen fail to recognise that he could be the assassin.

"You see it's a Brit, all cool and posh, acting like a devil," said Stirling, explaining the gag. "And it's all based on what is really happening right this moment in Sitcom Heaven. With any luck we'll get to splice in some real footage."

I did not notice anything mean, moody, politically astute or even remotely *Schindler's List*ish in any of this. Nor did the word "sensitive" come to mind.

"Can you do all that?" asked Stirling. "Cop Show Heaven style. Real cars. No safety net."

"Well as long as they're not real bullets I'm sure I can have a bash at it."

"No real bullets," said Stirling disappointedly. "I'll make a note of that."

I came to the conclusion that, crazed though Stirling was, it had not done his career any harm, in as much as he had a career where more sensible, sensitive, brilliant people never got off first base.

"Jump over this chair and show me something interesting," said Stirling backing away to make room for a spectacular stunt. "Go on. Give me some ideas."

I contemplated the swivel chair. It was a hefty device, not easily picked up. Even so I thought I might try a series of rolls with it. I might be able to incorporate a spin as well.

I warmed up a little. Removed my shoes and walked the area in which all this was to happen, making sure it was clear and then stood on the stool, dropped off it into a sitting position, and rolled backwards coming to a standing position leaving the stool in front.

Stirling gave a sigh.

"If you can afford to have me in hospital I'll do something more extravagant but right now I'm not even on the payroll."

"Good point," said Stirling. "I like you. What's your name?"

So that was how to get a big part with a superstar director! I felt excited. I loved it when I got a part in anything. It was usually after that when things got dull, but for the moment, I wallowed in the excitement.

The right thing to do, I decided was to phone up my writer, and inspire him. I wanted him to be busy writing a script that could get us both some serious US work. I imagined myself being played by a young Michael Caine. Or better still, a young Humphrey Bogart with an English accent! Or should that be, Cary Grant? Whoever it was, it would have to be a big and young major movie star of the moment.

"What?" said my writer, when I breathlessly gave him the news. "Who is this?"

"Pull out that old thriller script!" I said. "And get reworking it!"

"If this is some sick joke ..."

"I know I've been too busy to bother you lately," I wheedled. "But I'm calling you now. With inspiration!"

"I don't know what your game is," said my writer. "But stop wasting my time with these insane phone-calls! And you don't sound a bit like him by the way."

He slammed the phone down. Now, was that the sound of a writer binning his latest attempt, I wondered? All these years of me bringing that bastard easy money and this is how he treats me. I had a good mind to do something terrible like burn out the guy's fax machine. I had heard how you could loop a piece of black paper onto a fax machine and send it to someone you did not like. It would print out an entire roll of black paper and if you were lucky, have the machine burst into flames. I went off the idea when I realised how much this would cost long distance and decided to forget about it and tell Alice the good news.

I phoned her mobile and found her too busy to talk because, as she put it, she was standing up to her ankles in shit.

"This is what they call food preparation," she said. I could not get much sense out of her, so told her I would see her later on at The Pig Out.

Then Sydney phoned and in a very shaky voice asked whether I was feeling OK.

"The chicken feet old boy," said Sydney. "They are killers!"

Sydney told me he was dying on the toilet and if I wanted, I could listen to the sound of his stomach. For a few seconds I considered whether that slight knot in my own was merely part of the excitement of the day or the beginnings of cholera. Trust my luck that the moment I get anything good, I get something nasty.

When I met Lily at home, I had forgotten all about my good news and was feeling life-threatening twinges.

"Mm," she said. "Sounds like cholera to me. There's been an outbreak on the border."

Her mother was doing some article for *Cryogenic Weekly* and came across this phenomenon. It was a hot story and she was very pleased with herself.

"I can cure cholera though," said Lily, detecting my sickening complexion.

"I bet you can," I said, not doubting her restorative powers.

After a brief hesitation about the bathroom in case of disastrous intestinal explosions, I went off with Lily to examine the possibilities of faith.

When we popped up out of Gluttony Station and wandered around the exhaust-fume-laden streets in search of Lily's recommended medicine shop, I found myself plunged back from the edge of the electronic revolution to the depths of the darkest Middle Ages. Lily pointed out the bears' paws, tiger pizzles, and reindeer horn, all of which were supposed cures for impotence and decrepitude.

"Do they postpone or reduce it?"

"Both," assured Lily. "Though I suspect it is all a matter of degree. You for instance would probably do very well on this medicine."

"I don't think that department's much of a problem," I said sniffing the cloves, camphor and incense that blocked out the fumes of the street. By merely stepping through the door of the shop, I sensed that my sinuses had been cleansed.

The shop was not very busy and only an old man served behind the counter. He forewent the white coat in favour of the string vest and pyjama pants. He had the powdery complexion of rye bread and whole meal.

Lily explained why we were there. The old man's thin kindly smiling eyes rarely left off from looking at me.

He looked at my tongue, at my eyes, and took my pulse all at the same time. With a rough dismissal, the man began shovelling some twigs and leaf mould into a roll of brown paper.

"Just boil that stuff up and take a drink and that will clean your entire system."

"Isn't that what cholera does for you?"

"Yes, but that's a sickness. This is healthy."

I handed over a few dollars and thanked the old man for the brown package, which if anything smelt of liquorice.

Lily settled down for a long chat as the old man sipped a jam-jar of a urine-coloured concoction floating with leaves, twigs, and dead flowers. He kept looking at me and was much amused.

Finally, Lily took me by the hand and led me outside back into the thick humidity and smog of the crowded streets.

"He's my Grandfather," explained Lily. "My father's father. He's worth millions. He owns a big slab of Damnation and everyone wants it, so the value goes up and up but he refuses to sell."

I looked back at the scruffy little shop and wondered why anyone should hole themselves up there when they were reputably so rich.

"You never let go of what you have," said Lily.

I suddenly pulled my arm out of her hand.

"Nothing is going to happen between us," I said.

"Well of course not at home," said Lily. "That would be impossible and you will have to leave her."

"You are underage."

"Not for long," said Lily.

I ran across the road hoping that Lily would not follow. I kept running, pushing my way through the crowds, and eventually collapsed into the back seat of a taxi. The bobbing doll on the dashboard seemed to have a particularly malevolent grin on its face.

"The Pig Out," I said.

The driver's eyes, reflected in the rear-view mirror, brightened in recognition.

"Still here," said the driver.

"Oh yes," I said.

"And after next month?"

87

"I don't even know what is going to happen in the next ten minutes let alone the next month."

"Ah, we wait and see ha?"

"That's right, wait and see."

"And then you know why you really here?"

"Right now I wish I did know."

"Money, girls, being an unfashionable cliché ... those are the usual reasons."

When I arrived at The Pig Out, Alice was not there. I phoned her mobile and found an answering machine on the other end. This seemed a contradiction in terms. The whole point of having these phones was that one could be contacted at all times. I left a terse message and headed for the bar where I was immediately refused a drink for not being a member.

I searched for recognisable faces. I wanted to brag. I wanted to let people know that I had just landed a plum part in Stirling's movie. I wanted to forget Lily. I wanted to shag Lily, but I decided that I should shag someone entirely different. That way I could maintain audience interest, because they like nothing better than a sudden coupling of unlikely on-going characters. They thought they knew everything about them, and then suddenly ... they are in the sack together and several episodes can be spent unravelling the mystery of how they got there.

At last, I stumbled upon Cherry, who tried to ignore me but I begged her to use her temporary membership to get me a drink.

"So poor old Jake then, eh?" I said, talking about the love of her soap-opera life, as I gargled a half-pint of ice cold Guinness.

"He'll get over it," said Cherry.

"That's right," I said. "But why Jake? What had he that some toyboy like myself could not have willingly given you for much less hassle than an old sot like him?"

Cherry appeared flustered by this assault.

"It's a contradiction," I said. "That's what it is. Some great Brechtian contradiction that you draw upon for creative purposes. You just love to humiliate yourself with the ..."

"Shut up will you!" said Cherry.

"Look, it is absolutely necessary, having proved our dislike of each other, that we fall in love. It is the classic story."

"I don't even hate you. I'm indifferent to you," she said quoting the character profiles.

"Shame, because I thought just how nice it would be for me to introduce you to one of the guys involved with all those shootings in Sitcom Heaven."

Cherry closed her eyes and I could see her brain ticking as she was working out just how despicable I was.

"What shootings?"

"Haven't you heard? It's been in the papers. Stirling's basing his movie on them. I thought you could do a little profile on me in Cop Show Heaven."

"What are you talking about?"

"I could let you meet up with some of the stunt guys round here. They're being pulled into this Sitcom thing. It's a turf war over loan sharking and gambling deals …"

"That's the movie, is it?"

"No! That's the thing it's being based on. You really should listen to the local news. You see, half the police there are devils and now they have to take sides in the realignment of power. It's raw power politics. Something to make your coverage of Cop Show Heaven a little juicier than the usual stuff."

"That's the plot of your movie. What is the real news?"

I was not sure what my real news was, but whatever real news there was, it was sure to be known by Fizzy, and Fizzy and Cherry had names that really did fit together.

*

"You're what?" said Fizzy.

Fizzy was picking his teeth, his phone on the table before him. And about him squat little women with black curly hair, big rubber aprons, and sloshing gum boots busily pushed trolleys of eels and oysters up and down a thin corridor between tin shacks.

Cherry and I were visiting him at a little seaside squatter encampment built by fishing folk and old gargoyles. The chief businesses were oyster drying and restaurants catering to the surrounding housing-development residents and container-terminal workers. The clatter of mah-jong tiles, the stench of drying fish, the flies and the bubbling woks and wicker baskets of rotting vegetation overwhelmed us. I imagined that at any moment we would be slit up the gills and filleted.

Fizzy picked at his teeth some more with a slither of tooth pick, then spat it out onto the pile of eviscerated crab shells and shrimp heads that lay before him attracting the flies.

The beach area comprised several hundred years of accumulated oyster shell debris interspersed with mud and the dilapidated hulls of long dead fishermen's boats. It was an excellent place for a bloody battle. The shells were razor sharp. To drag someone through this was to rip the flesh off their face and create just the right bloody image for a good hero to recover from and then find the angry strength to put together the right mental outlook to create the *Bone Softening Fist*. Then with a somersault delivery in the place designated by the Feng Shui Man, all foes would be vanquished.

"You're what? Doing a film with Stirling?" he said. "He will never be able to shoot here."

"Why not," I asked.

"Because I say he won't," said Fizzy. "And you had better stay clear of him."

"Fizzy," I said, sensing that Cherry was beginning to look at her watch and wonder when she was going to be able to get what she was after, "we're friends, me and you. I'm doing you many favours. I'm looking after your interests."

"And I will look after yours when the time comes, but you will be betraying me if you work with Stirling."

"Maybe I can smooth things over between you. It's only money that's the problem isn't it? You want him to use your people. Isn't that what it's about?"

"You have a word with him. You make him understand what is required."

"I'll try," I said. "I'm sure something can be sorted out. In the meantime, allow me to introduce you to my good friend."

Fizzy had noticed Cherry and allowed his leering eyes to fix on her cleavage. Cherry, however, made a blunder by putting her cassette recorder on the table. Fizzy immediately switched it off.

"There's no need to be melodramatic," I said, with an easy informality that visibly made all the other crew-members, knocking back their beer and slurping down their steamed prawns, shudder.

I began to understand that Fizzy was on duty. He thus required a lot of face to be able to control some of these tattooed, broken-toothed characters.

"Quick, offer to sleep with the man," I said, nudging Cherry. "Let him show you what an Asian action hero in his prime can do."

Before Cherry could tell me to go and do something obscene, I gave her a quick kick under the table that made all the crew laugh out loud.

"OK," said Cherry. "No recordings. No names. I would like some of the background to the troubles in Sitcom Heaven and how this will be reflected here in Cop Show Heaven."

"You understand that you could have your arms chopped off," said Fizzy. "Probably they chop other bits of you off as well and throw them in the harbour. You understand?"

I explained how last year an editor had his arm chopped off for mentioning the secret name of God in his magazine.

"I'm not trying to get anyone arrested," said Cherry. "I'm merely trying to get some perspective on this place."

"The Devil is going to come in here big," said Fizzy. "So Cop Show Heaven will not be like Sitcom Heaven. But those across the border, they still want a piece of the action. So they come and rob our jewellers and our banks and shoot our policemen. But a deal is done with local Dragon Heads. When they get to know things, in exchange for the heat being taken off them, they whisper in the right ear and these outsiders find themselves ambushed. But it's not like that in Sitcom Heaven. There the border is all around. It is a little place and people slip in and out and the police … well, which police? One lot will not fight to protect the interests of some other lot. Understand? Cop Show Heaven protects its own. Sitcom Heaven is a free for all. That's why they could throw the bomb at the governor."

"That sounds very reassuring," said Cherry.

Fizzy looked puzzled at Cherry's comment.

"It's irony," I explained. "She means exactly the opposite."

Fizzy then laughed and explained why he was laughing to his men who all joined in.

Fizzy continued, "There are armies you see. They see weaknesses in certain areas so are moving to grab them. New people, with connections in Hell, who claim they are patriots and bringing stability. See?"

Fizzy rubbed his thumb and forefinger together indicating money would have to change hands.

"What happens in Sitcom Heaven will make a difference, but we are confident."

Cherry jotted this down and I thought how clever she must be to follow all that. Then the rain stopped and the crew became active. They would have to move very quickly if they were to get the shot in.

As Fizzy sloshed through the mud and fish heads, he glad-handed old men wearing vests rolled up over their pot bellies, with flip-flops on their feet, slipping rolls of money into the palms of their hands. As camera and sound equipment were quickly manhandled along the corridor, Cherry and I followed on to take a glimpse at the oyster beach. Fizzy grabbed my arm and waved Cherry on.

"You don't fuck about. Understand? Remember the deal. You and Alice. Right?"

"I know," I said. "But Alice is very busy at the moment."

"And look after my daughter."

"Why don't you look after her?" I said. "I hate to say this Fizzy, but I have not seen you spend much quality time with her."

Fizzy looked angry for a moment and then playfully tapped me on the cheek and grinned.

"That's right, Dan," he said. "But I'm busy too."

With that understanding reached, Fizzy rushed through to the beach, with its oyster shells and sea rotted plastic bags and bottles swept upon the shore by the last storm. Cherry did not look too impressed.

"Let's get out of this dump," she said.

"Don't you want to see the evil bad guy have his face ripped off?"

"I think I can give that a miss."

Cherry gave a nod of acknowledgement to Fizzy as we left.

"What did I tell you?" I said. "He's great isn't he? An original?"

"Morally reprehensible I would say," said Cherry.

Cherry turned the ignition and hit the air-conditioner.

"You think it's somehow hip to mix with him."

"Hey, I'm just a stock cop show character. I have to work where I can."

For the most part of the journey we were silent. I thought how mixing sex with violence was pleasurable.

"Have you thought of that profile of me then," I said, hoping I sounded sufficiently cheerful and positive to wipe away any of the ingratitude that Cherry was currently exhibiting.

"Yes," said Cherry. "I thought of doing a sort of *Where are they now*? You know, how low can you sink sort of thing?"

I climbed out of the car and Cherry drove off. The cheek of this woman! I gave her such a good interview as well. I had a good mind to make sure that Edward got a transcript.

I could see the column now: "Dan Symmons, currently starring in a new Lance Stirling movie, was telling me all about how Cop Show Heaven's underworld saw the transition as a means to a fast buck."

I popped into the marbled halls where Edward was staying and phoned through to his room.

"Hi Ed," I said. "Aren't you up and sober yet?"

Edward was up and had been writing, so was looking for distraction. He agreed to meet me in the coffee lounge and I arrived with a photographer. I introduced him, then ordered coffees and chatted for a while. I, a little edgy in the presence of the surly photographer with the face of ageless evil, bragged about my new part and how I had some interesting things to tell Edward.

"You should be checking out the Sitcom Heaven scene," I said. "Cherry's putting together a great story. You wouldn't want her to beat you."

"Oh god," said Edward. "It's irrelevant. I've been chasing up on some Heavenly grumblings about God handing over the names of Cop Show Heaven subversives to the Devil."

"They'll let you publish that?"

"Maybe," said Edward. "People complain about *The Post*'s Hellish minders, but that's nothing compared to the workings of the old boy network back home. So I've got a few lighter pieces on the go."

At that point, the photographer asked me to oblige him with a few snaps. Of course I obliged. I posed in my chair looking sufficiently windswept and interesting, or at least as much as one can in the coffee lounge of a luxury hotel. As the photographer snapped away, he told me how he featured in many British dramas on the death of Princess Diana. He was the guy who used to spend his time trying to shoot up Princess Diana's skirt to give the great British public a glimpse of her knickers. "We had her tits once," he said. "But that's as far as we got."

"It's a pity she's not wrapping up the flag in Cop Show Heaven then."

"Yeah, we were hoping Prince Charles would get knocked off and end up in one of Hell's brothels. Or at least someone who looks a lot like him. I mean, otherwise who gives a fucking toss about Cop Show Heaven going to Hell?"

"Certainly no-one who isn't a fictional character it would seem."

"Precisely. But if it all goes arse up and there's a good massacre, the cultural fall out in the western world will give various heads of state a real problem."

"Teenage boys will take to vandalism and masturbation?"

"England will have its culture from America and its money from Europe. There'll be nothing fucking decent and tasteful ever again. Mind I think it's all fucked forever even if nothing tasty with a few tanks happens here."

"What a shame."

"I'm only here for the beer anyway."

I tried to look relaxed and cool as the camera popped and whirred, though there seemed to be a few too many pictures being taken and the photographer prowled about me like he was stalking some particularly poisonous snake.

"This'll be part of an article I'm calling Surprise Meetings," said Edward. "It's a lighter piece than the usual. A sort of *Where are they now* piece. You know, minor TV characters in limbo …"

I screwed up my eyes and flinched at another flash from the camera.

"Nice one," said the photographer. "Move your arse a bit."

"Just stop that for a moment," I said. "I want to check that article for misinformation."

"I don't think there is any," said Edward. "You've been trying to get some Kung Fu parts haven't you?"

"No," I said. "I am being developed as the main character in a Hollywood movie."

"Then it'll be egg all over my face when I publish this."

"Yes it will be."

The photographer took another photo, this time with me suffering from a bad squint.

"Tasty!"

CHAPTER FIVE

I began to doubt that Stirling existed. I knew that I was overstating my position when I said this was a Hollywood Movie, but it was by a dead director who had done Hollywood stuff. I would be as much of a star in this as I had been in any of my TV work. Only nobody was very impressed. What did they know anyway? I would turn my own hype into reality.

I took the subway to Stirling's restaurant in the hope of catching the man in and reassuring myself that it was all very real. I could have phoned him but there was always that fear I would be told Stirling was in a meeting when I knew perfectly well that for Stirling, there were no meetings.

On arrival I peered through the glass in the door and hesitated. What if it was all a joke? No, I was the man's best friend, buddy, bosom pal, and leading actor and there had been no reason why Stirling could not have chosen any other star. To have been chosen by Stirling was proof of one's star quality. Except I did not feel like a star. It all felt a little too easy, no contract had been signed, and since being told that I had the part, I had heard nothing. Enter then I must, and puffing up my ego and my smile, I burst through the door, waved away the waiter asking me if I had reservations – "More than you can imagine, darling!" – and went through to the back office to clarify my status.

I caught Stirling lying back in a vibrating chair while talking long distance.

"Oooh," he kept saying to whoever was on the end of the phone. "We've got to get a chair like this back home. Though I think I'll try and get one without surgical pink foot rollers."

Stirling saw me and gestured me to hang on a minute while he finished his call.

"Ciao for now and lots of blue kisses, haaa!" he said and switched the phone off. "Have you had a go on one of these things?" he said, getting up and giving me a chance to experience the comforts of an automatic foot rub and neck kneed.

"Wonderful in its gruesomeness," said Stirling grabbing hold of some magazine cuttings. "Here's more wonderful stuff," he said thrusting them under my nose. "I've been doing research.

Have you read this about Sitcom Heaven? Brigadier Manuel Soares Mange, their security chief, says, "These are professional killers, they never miss." And that's why it's safe for tourists! The guy's an ass-hole."

"I think that's Civic Pride talking."

"Haa, too right Danny Boy. But they sure are getting a lot of practice in. Listen to this ..."

Stirling left me shivering on the vibrating lounger and ransacked his desk for highlighted news paragraphs.

I guess this is the difference between dead directors and their imagined characters. They are interested in the real world, whereas we are what the real world is interested in.

"April. Dismembered body found in two nylon bags. The head had been boiled in a corrosive liquid. Lam Pui Chang is gunned down in a car park. Lee Chi Wong joins rampage in arcade, chopping and stabbing teenagers. After a molotov cocktail explodes, police arrive with guns blazing and Lee goes down. Rosa Yiu Bo La – sounds like some horrible virus, don't she? Anyway, she's shot getting into her car. She was a nice person, says a friend, but that doesn't stop you getting murdered. May: Three alleged Hell Fire Club members are sprayed with bullets in their car outside the National Bank of Hell in revenge for Lam Pui Chang. Crazy Ng Biu is snuffed in a toilet at the Pung Key Seafood Restaurant, said to be a hangout for loan sharks. His two attackers flee on motorbikes. June: two prostitutes disappear in the President Hotel. Three fingers, complete with nail polish, are found in the sewer beneath the hotel. Two heads to match are later discovered below an embankment on Disney Island. It goes on ... And they say that *Movies* are violent!"

I finally managed to switch the chair off and sit up. The office seemed still to be moving but it was only Stirling. His eyes were viewing some personal movie in which blood was splattering the walls.

"We'll have you pushing someone head first into a bubbling wok and the head sizzling and the guy screaming and running around with his head fried and the skin breaking off like crackling and the eyes hanging out and the blackened ears ..."

Stirling came to a shuddering halt as he realised that I was not very taken with this creative vision.

"It's what's happening, Dan. We've got to reflect that. We've got to be truthful."

"I suppose so."

"Heaven is like an onion," said Stirling holding his fist before him and beginning to peel off the fingers. "Layer upon layer until you get to the evil core that makes everything else possible."

Stirling was struck with this image.

"Evil as a necessity," he said. "That's the theme. Without it, all you get is the cuckoo clock."

"I'm not sure I follow," I said.

"Orson Wells in *The Third Man*. Switzerland has a thousand years of peace and gives the world the cuckoo clock while everyone else beats the shit out of each other and gives us the Renaissance. Something like that."

"Aren't Swiss banks supposed to have stolen lots of gold and stuff from victims of the Nazis?"

"Well there you are," said Stirling. "Even they had evil at the heart … That's the Title: EVIL AT THE HEART!"

Stirling scribbled it down on a note-pad.

"I'll fax that through to the writer. This calls for a complete rewrite. Have you seen the script so far? Piece of shit. He'll rewrite before he gets the last payment. We are going to have to go down a different road on this one."

"Maybe you should have brought him out here to soak up the atmosphere."

"What? Have the writer know more about my movie than I do? You gotta be kidding. Better that I soak up the atmosphere and tell him what it is than have the little toad creeping about here wanting to write my movie. He'd only get drunk and get the clap and want to write about karaoke lounge hostesses. Let your writers get laid and they lose it. Anyway, what are you here for?"

"I thought I would see how the contract was coming along."

"Haven't you got it yet? I'll get onto my lawyer. Who's your agent?"

"I'm between agents."

"Use mine. Here's my card. I'll get him onto it right away. Bastard will negotiate you a big increase."

"They won't have a conflict of interest?"

"What? They screw ten percent out of what they get for both *me and you*. They'd rather see the money in their pockets than on the screen. The only loser here will be the movie."

I did not want to investigate this logic too closely. Instead, I had a task to perform. I wanted certainty, and I thought I had better pass on Fizzy's message, just in case I ever needed Fizzy to help me again.

"Are you sure you're going to be able to shoot this thing?" I said. "Because ... er ... I've been talking to some interested parties and they tell me that you won't deal with them."

"Who've you been talking to?"

"Fizzy Tang."

"Fizzy Tang! He's nobody."

"I don't know. He seems to have connections with some of the guys you've been talking about."

"Listen, if I pay him what he wants, then some other tin-pot little outfit will start muscling in on me saying that Fizzy is a piece of shit and that they will take him and me out. Pretty soon I'm paying off *everyone* for so-called location rights. Frankly, I can film anywhere I please and I don't need these guys to smooth my way."

My portable phone began to ring.

"Jesus!" said Stirling, clasping his heart. "Bloody phones in this town. I swear in the cinema half the audience is talking to the other half on their telephones."

It was Fizzy.

"I was just talking about you," I said.

"Who to?" said Fizzy.

"To ... er ... Lance," I said, "Lance Stirling. Do you want to talk to him?"

"No," said Fizzy. "Tell him he's dead if I don't play."

"He's dead if he don't play," I repeated out loud.

"I'll play with him alright," said Stirling. "Better not tell him that. He won't recognise irony. Just tell him I don't do business like this."

"He won't do business like this," I said.

"We won't do business at all then," said Fizzy. "Tell him that."

"You tell him."

"I don't want to talk to him. I want to talk to *you*. Fuck Stirling."

"What do you want to talk to me about?"

"I want you to go rescue Lily."

"What's she done now?"

"Nothing yet. Just find her before the police lock her up, OK?"

"This would be a good time for you to do some active parenting," I suggested.

"I am, I'm sending you to stop her fucking about."

"I don't think I'm really the best person to send. I think you should send someone else. Anyone else ..."

But the phone had already gone dead.

I looked at Stirling who was giving me a withering stare.

"I'm on the payroll of another project," I said sheepishly.

"You'd better not let it clash with your responsibilities to me," said Stirling.

"Oh no," I said rising from the chair. "Don't you worry about that. I know exactly where my priorities lie. Nice chair by the way."

"Yeah," said Stirling settling back into it. "Imagine having a fuck in one of these. No effort required. Dangle the girl on your dick and then varoom ... fast, slow, and even with a circular motion ..."

I left Stirling playing with the controls and hurried into the heat of the night. As I fingered the business card Stirling had given me, I felt confident again. One minute you are up in this town and then you are down and then up again. I felt an involuntary shiver. Whether this was the fear of failure, the hatred of uncertainty or the sudden realisation that I was off to see Lily again, I was not sure. What I did know was that seeing Lily again was not a good idea.

My avowed intention of keeping on the good side of Fizzy just in case I needed him at some future date did not quite fall in with my suspicion that the next meeting with Lily would end up with me playing hide the sausage. Fizzy, a person whose potential for violence was only just dawning upon me, was not going to take my sleeping with the precious daughter very well. However, I had promised him that I would go and look after the girl.

Actually, I had not promised any such thing. Fizzy had merely assumed that I would.

So, which was the least bad option to take? Break my promise to Fizzy, not roger his daughter, get my neck broken? Or, not break my promise to Fizzy, roger his daughter, get my neck broken?

I stepped out onto the road and grabbed a taxi. As I climbed in I phoned Lily and over the crackly line, I could hear shouts and the unmistakable sounds of civil discord.

"Yeah?" said Lily.

"Hi there," I said. "Where are you?"

"Victory Park. We've put up the Pillar of Shit in commemoration of all the evil in the world."

"I'll be there right away!" I said.

"You have to show your support," she said.

"That's right," I said.

She told me where I could find her then complained that she did not have time to talk on the phone. Then there were shouts and the line went dead.

"Lily?" I said.

"Uh?" said the taxi-driver.

I leaned forward and looked for the Buddha, but no, nothing more than a fluffy air perfumer was stuck to the dashboard and the driver was a thickset thuggish looking man with one eye.

"Doesn't that make it hard driving around here?" I asked.

"What?"

"Nothing," I said.

"Nothing?"

The driver swivelled half round in his seat and give me a squinty look with his one eye and then grinned and nodded and muttered, "One eye helps you concentrate, idiot!"

'Idiot?' I thought, and maybe I was. My mood was difficult to pin down. Events were overtaking me. Others were making all the decisions and I was merely being dragged along, or was it dragged down? I was not sure which and not at all sure that I liked it, but there was not much else I could do. If I wanted to be a developed character, I had to go with the flow. If not, I would remain an unfashionable stereotype.

I arrived at The Park where preparations for the evening's vigil were still in progress. The rain had obviously held things up. Nevertheless, the stage was being set and the microphones were being tested. Already a crowd was gathering.

As a park, it did not look much. It mostly consisted of tennis and basketball courts, as far as I could make out. The statue of God in the centre had the nose of a pug boxer and suspiciously red streaks of paint. This spoke of a previous year's assault by an artist making his personal statement on the handover and, as far as I could gather, his lack of support by the local council's arts budget.

In the light of what I thought a suitably mad artistic statement, I decided that I should phone Alice.

"I thought I might stay here and see if there were any of the press about for me to explain a few things to," I said.

"They'll only say you're some washed up nobody trying to muscle back into the limelight by saving the world. I'd give them a miss if I was you."

Alice hung up and did not even say whether she would be coming along later.

"Woooooo!" said a voice and I turned to see Lily dressed in a white gown.

"Like a ghost, huh?" She pulled out a handful of candles and handed some to me. "For later on," she explained and gave a wave back at some of her friends, passing with their candles and mourning clothes at the ready. I recognised the Die Nasty bunch.

"They're going to try get onto the platform to sing a few songs," explained Lily. "Either that or sell a few of their CDs to the crowd."

"Oh," I said, certain that she was wearing very little under the white smock, especially as the rain began to fall and cause it to cling to her body.

She put up an umbrella and put her arm about my waist.

"I hope you've been thinking about my birthday," said Lily. "I notice you and mother haven't been together much."

"That's got nothing to do with you," I said.

"I know, it's got more to do with her and Padget," said Lily. "He's a very boring person. I really hate him. He's always so smug and whiny. I think he must have been begging her or something. That's the only reason I can think why they've got back together."

"What are you trying to tell me?"

"You don't mean to say you don't know?"

I did not know, but now I did.

The crowd thickened and the stage began to fill with those who were going to speak, sing, and recite poetry. The rain stopped and there was a murmur of approval as the umbrellas came down.

"We're going to get a great turn-out tonight," said Lily, giving her smock a quick airing.

As the evening progressed, songs and poems were sung and poemed, though nothing from Die Nasty, who managed to get into a fistfight with the security team. Their CDs were confiscated, promptly pirated and several thousand copies were exported to Hell in twelve hours flat. Prayers were offered and peace doves, then the candles, and the torch of democracy lit. The air crackled with sobs, laughter, jeers, and cheers when appropriate.

I felt that I was in a character defining moment. History was playing out with me as part of it. Strangely, at the same time, waves of frustration came over me, just as I imagine real people suffer. The flickering candles then reminded me of my back-story, of Christmas, of childhood. They threw my mind back to feelings of magical possibilities that had translated themselves into filthy adult things that were not the source of the happiness I had always imagined. I did not know what that source was: hope, imagination, and belief in miracles? I did not know! But here in the night with a clear sky, with a beautiful girl, with a mass of flickering candles and a crowd of people exercising a moment of self-deception, believing that they could have everything, that happiness could be ever after, I knew it was a lie, but it was beautiful.

Now if that was not a piece of self-realisation above and beyond the requirements of a character from a popular TV show in a post-Christian society, I do not know what was.

Just when the evening was melting into a perfect moment, Lily excused herself saying that she had to help with taking the Pillar of Shit over to The University because the authorities would not let it stay in the park.

"I really feel we are making our point," said Lily, giving me a heart-melting grin, then a quick kiss. "I take it that you've changed your mind?" she said.

"Yes, of course," I said, hoping that she meant I had changed my mind about not taking advantage of her and ruining her life.

"We'll talk later."

Then she ran off with some other youngsters. They all looked like fourteen-year-old angels from a nativity play in their Nikes and white smocks and made me feel even more like an aged pederast.

I tried to run after her but the police had already forced the demonstrators to bundle the Pillar into the back of a lorry which was now trundling out of the park with Lily perched on the back chanting, "Welcome Reunion, Fight for Democracy!"

I supposed only Hell could really be a Democracy. With God in Heaven, which is supposedly perfect, who needs a vote?

I became swamped by the dispersing crowds and struggled to find a taxi. I was terrified that Lily would get herself arrested again, especially since I was supposed to be there to stop that from happening.

By the time I reached the university, I found that I had missed a near riot. The university authorities had refused to let the students put the statue on the campus. Since they had been ordered out of the park by the police and were now being ordered off the campus by the same police, tempers had become frayed and a considerable amount of pushing and shoving had ensued.

Lily, I feared, was more than likely to have been in the midst of it, and I pictured her being dragged off and thrown into the back of a police van. And all for what? I thought the statue an odd piece of literalism.

The police however, were now everybody's friends. In their green uniforms and caps, they posed for photographs beside the students, shaking hands, grinning from ear to ear, and standing before the truck that contained the three dismantled pieces of the offending statue. A compromise had been reached. So long as the statue remained in the truck, in its three pieces, it could remain on campus until a more suitable place for its display could be found.

When I found Lily, she sported a bruise above her eye and had a hoarse voice from shouting but she was very jolly, declaring they had had a victory. "They capitulated," she said and grabbed hold of my arm.

"But it remains in the truck," I said.

"But we'll find somewhere to put it," said Lily. "Besides, it shows that the police are on our side as it is. They told us so. Only ..."

"Only it's a piece of shit?"

"Well, we're not qualified to make that sort of judgement. But it is meant to be provocative."

"I guess that's enough then," I said.

"This is not the time to talk about aesthetics. This is the time to make a stand."

"And the police agreed with you?"

"Oh yes," she said. "They said they would help find a place to put it."

"Isn't that a bit like your mum and dad liking the same music as you?"

"I don't understand."

"There's no point if your mum and dad like it! So you have to find something even more outrageous."

"I think that must be a human thing," said Lily.

"I think it must be."

*

Silent in the back of the taxi, a Chinese God of Wealth dangled from the mirror and Lily and I held hands. If the police could be fourteen years old, I certainly could be sixteen. And how old is a fictional character anyway – especially if they have not been written yet? I was never born, I just sort of am, but just not quite yet. It all allows a certain amount of leeway regarding age-related behaviour and legal ages of consent, and in the end my age would depend upon the actor who was cast to play me anyway.

Back at the apartment, Lily put on the kettle for a pot of noodles and some tea and we prepared to separate and head for our respective bedrooms. Alice was bound to be back any time now and she would have to be tackled in a discrete manner.

"Maybe I should pack and go find a hotel room," I suggested.

"I could come with you!"

"You're under age," I said, wondering what on earth had happened to me. This would not have stopped the Dan I used to know.

"My birthday's next month," said Lily, giving me a kiss.

I felt an overwhelming urge to bang my head against the wall but forewent the pleasure as Alice returned looking flustered and nervous. Lily asked her if she felt OK but all she said was go to bed and get out of those morbid clothes. As far as I could see, the white smock was a creative success.

Lily backed off and gave me a little wave before disappearing with her noodle bowl to her room.

"We've been to the massacre commemoration," I said.

"Yeah, well I missed it," said Alice, heading for her bedroom.

I followed and stood awkwardly by the door.

"I think this is getting boring," said Alice. "You've become dull and predictable."

"Uhuh?"

"We've had a run for our money," said Alice. "But I am in the business of tidying up my life and you are not tidy."

"You just said I was dull and predictable."

"And untidy. You leave unwashed spoons all over the place. You drip coffee into the sugar. You throw newspapers onto the floor and never pick them up."

I thought that I was relatively unslovenly but I was not going to argue, since this was all a prelude to some great face-saving revelation that could free both of us.

"I know Fizzy had great hopes for you," said Alice. "But I don't want him ruling either of our lives."

"I never took any of that seriously."

"If he really wants Lily to move in with him, he should ask her. She's old enough to know what she wants."

"I did suggest that to him."

"He likes to own people. But he doesn't matter to me."

"Who does?"

"Look I think you should sleep on the sofa tonight and we'll talk about this in the morning."

"I take it there is someone then?"

Alice avoided looking me in the eye.

"It's OK," I said. "In fact this situation is not that unusual for me. It normally doesn't take this long."

I quickly began collecting things from the bedroom and stuffing them into my suitcase.

"You don't have to be so bloody cheerful about it!" said Alice.

"I'm not," I said. "Only I've got a starring part in Stirling's film and life seems to be getting back in order again. So what made you and Padgett patch it up then? I take it, it is this Padgett character?"

"He explained how Lily had come on to him and well, I thought, may be, judging by the way she was coming onto you, it was her way of getting rid of everyone. She's like her father in that she wants to own everyone."

I had never thought of this possibility.

"She's not coming on to me!"

"Oh, she is. She is so obvious about it. She does it to everyone who even comes near me."

This depressed me.

That night as I tried to become comfortable upon the sofa, I vowed to do myself a favour and leave early in the morning before Lily could get up and warp my judgement.

*

"Yes," said Sydney. "You are better out of any relationship with a Lolita character. They'll only cast you as Jeremy Irons."

I had met Sydney for lunch in a noodle shop round the corner from the 20th Century hotel. My hotel was not cheap, but for the moment it would have to do until I got hold of an apartment. Sydney had promised to put his in-law connections to work finding me a temporary residence for a reasonable price in one of their many apartments bought for speculative reasons.

Sydney warned me that once you are mixed up with a family your life stops being your own. Favours pile up and soon, like everyone else in Cop Show Heaven, you are sucked into having to do the right thing by everyone.

"Including your mistresses," I added, just so that Sydney did not forget that half his problems were of his own making.

"I used to think," said Sydney, mournfully, "that being a fictional character was to change the consciousness of people and make a difference. In fact, it makes bugger all difference. Prozac! Now that makes a difference! And much more effectively. But being imaginary is a complete waste of one's life."

I thought Sydney was looking a little fraught.

"Put it down to the handover jitters old chap," said Sydney, ordering another bottle of Divine Light beer and lighting up a cigarette. "I've decided to take up smoking again. I feel there's little future for me here, or anywhere else for that matter. Still, the depression will no doubt pass. Especially if property prices hit the roof."

If Sydney was worried about the handover, not to mention all his women, perhaps I should also be worried. There was always a chance of some bloody disaster.

As I took my leave, I sauntered out into the humid air and tried to square the hordes that I saw going about their shopping with the impending doom and disaster. In the movies, periods like this would consist of sharp cuts to beating drums, armbands, proclamations being slapped on fading brickwork, and political demonstrations being broken up by brown-shirted thugs.

I visited The Pig Out hoping that there was the possibility of meeting Lily, even if she was a bitch cow manipulator of male genetic code. Nevertheless, she was not there that moment and to phone her would be to fall into her trap.

Die Nasty had just finished a set on the stage, capitalising on the sudden fame the bootleg of their album had brought them, and were propping up the bar.

"Do you know what a stupid name your band has?" I said.
"Do you know what stupid names everyone has on this planet?"

The band drank hefty pints of Divine Light and spoke of how they first met in The University's Refectory.

When their second set came up, I was lubricated enough to join them on stage, singing *Stairway to Heaven* and then, on discovering they also loved old Sixties anthems, joined them in a heavy rock version of *Hey Big Spender*.

So successful was my Shirley Bassey impersonation that I did a few requests and went into Liza Minnelli singing *Liza with a Zee*, complete with cute hand gestures, bumps and grinds. I borrowed a boa from one of the audience for added authenticity. After *I like to be in America*, both the male and female parts, I launched into *Don't Cry For Me Argentina* and created a sensation by being the first Friday Night open mike act to be applauded.

Mad Mick, an otherwise ordinary looking bloke with a beer gut, a waistcoat, and a bow-tie, pushed through the crowd and handed me his card. He put together variety shows (Mick's Bag of All Sorts) for various restaurants and thought that a good drag act would be just the thing. He was particularly keen on getting in someone to do a full Last Supper, complete with a St Mary impersonation.

"And if you can juggle yer tits," he added, "all the better."

Upon that I showed what I could do with three empty beer bottles, and was assured that I would have an enormous future in Hell.

"They are starved of any live entertainment there," said Mick, "The money's not enormous, but it is always there. And tax free."

So I had a future, no matter what.

A week later, an offending little article crept into Heaven's News about derelict cop-show characters. It featured a half page photograph of me naked to the waist with my lips rouged, the boa around my neck and a pint mug in my hand.

"Dan Simons, (sic) disgraced TV character, finds his own level," said the caption. The story made me out to be some sort of primitive, unfit to be admitted to Heaven proper.

"To think I used to have to jump off the pavement when they passed by," said one taxi-driver. "Now I have to step over them."

The writer was Cherry Halligan.

Fuck her, I thought, and vowed to renew my harassing of her when I caught up with her again.

*

With immense pleasure, I rose at four o'clock in the morning to be picked up by Stirling's mini-bus and taken to the first location. Dawn was beautiful on Mount Sinai. One of the mildewed mansions, one of the very few still with walls and passable windows, was requisitioned and the grounds tidied up to give the illusion of colonial splendour. Here was to be a simple scene to help break in the characters. It was a cocktail party with beautiful people dressed as only Cop Show Heaven can be dressed. Here the glittering colonial establishment was to swan about with champagne in hand bitching about the natives and worrying about their investments.

Here the audience was to learn there were some endangered dissidents in need of whisking away before the devils hit them with an attack of Triad hit men. A possible bomb under the atomic power station was also being worked into the plot.

I had a bad haircut so that I would look like everyone else, and was tucked inside a very hot tuxedo. I did my main shots in one take, leaving endless retakes to the scenes featuring the extras who seemed to be a poor bunch of imports from a bad night at The Pig Out. This bunch seemed irrationally of much the same age, and after a few glasses of champagne had forgotten they were on a film set and were not supposed to bunch together and giggle.

Stirling tried to tell them that they should each have some sort of objective at this party. They were supposed to be circulating. Some wanted to get laid and others to make contacts for business purposes and so on. However, the extras were not listening. They were there for the laugh and the more natural they got, the more wooden they appeared.

Perhaps the controlled chaos of the set was a little less controlled than I was used to but I did not fret, my future was assured. The film would be wonderful. I had a great sex scene with a number of young nymphomaniacs to look forward to. I was going to give them a lot of tongue.

"I'm so glad I got you Dan," said Stirling. "You are going to be the saviour of this movie. Your performance is just ... great!"

"I'd like to see the rushes," I said.

"No," said Stirling, "I never show the rushes. It can distort a performance. Just keep doing what you do and we'll get through this."

Low-budget movie making creates a siege mentality. It is not a job of work but a military campaign, a battle against time and money. Stirling was beginning to suffer from the strain but I was in my element. I entertained everyone on set, though none of them were happy, for they hated the heat and the rain and they thought the devils were about to swarm across the border and hack them to pieces. I kept telling them that everything was cool, that everything was going to be fine, and that there was nothing to fear.

At night, I dreamt of how I would conduct my life in Hollywood. I would fly into town on the tails of the film. I would go on a promotional tour. I would be the latest star. I would be big and my actor would have a beach house in Malibu, attend Danny DeVito's Fourth of July Party, meet Madonna, visit Michael Jackson ... maybe not Michael Jackson. Either way, there was an outrageous life-style coming my way. I would bring glamour back to the town. I would bring out the screaming fans and the rapacious autograph hunters. I would set the place alive with a frenzy unseen since the first days of the talkies. Tail fins and pink cadillacs, scarves and dark glasses, strawberry blondes and poodles, popcorn and gala performances would fill my days, my bed, and my veins. There would be no limits to shallowness and bad taste. Trophy boys, trophy girls would swim through my swimming pools, posing and preening, and soaking up enormous amounts of semen. White powder would go up my nose, up my bum, into my arm and I would stagger like no raddled old icon had staggered before, to be rehabilitated at a Betty Ford clinic like no-one else had ever been rehabilitated. Oprah Winfrey would preside. The stratosphere of fame and fortune would beckon. A private plane would take me wherever I wished. A private amusement park, a private zoo, a private planet would host me and my hangers-on. Designers would not have labels except for those that I wore ... I would be Human. I would be real. I would be the actor because he would be chosen to be me. No longer would I be merely a dream.

To sleep on such dreams served only to boost my adrenaline. When the great Kung Fu scene came where I had to pretend to do a death-defying leap through the window of a passing tram, I was primed, I was steaming, I was determined to get it all done in one take. If it were not done in one take, it would mean that I had missed and broken my neck. Nevertheless, I was game for the greater glory of a future of life embroiled in the business of increasing the world's trivia overload.

However, the rain kept postponing the day. The impossible two-week shoot was thankfully extended to four weeks as Stirling broke his own rules and put his own money into the production. This left the production straddling the handover celebrations, which Stirling decided to incorporate into the whole proceedings using three cameras.

The story in this last scene was a chase sequence through the crowds, where I ran to grab the kidnapped love of my life, who was being dragged away at gun point by the frustrated villain. The villains were to be caught up with as the fireworks popped, the flags changed and the policemen swapped their truncheons for tridents.

Stirling hoped, that with lots of real footage, they would be able to use this sequence to pad out an extra five minutes of movie. That would make the whole thing a more respectable length, especially since some of those early scenes on Mount Sinai were so awful that they had cut them down to their bare bones.

"We haven't any more money," Stirling told me. "We'd better get this or else the crew walks."

I was primed. On a couple of occasions I also hit The Pig Out on Friday Night with Mick's Bag of All Sorts, doing a quick drag act where I never came out of character and billed myself as Lu Lu so that Stirling would not find out. I did it for the laugh rather than anything else, though I found it slightly unnerving when, on the last performance, Fizzy, Mr Ng and Mr Kwok arrived and whooped it up, lifting my skirts. Then Fizzy twigged and followed me to the communal dressing room and berated me for dressing up like that.

"If you allow me to undress," I said, "then I won't offend your sensibilities any more, though I didn't see any qualms before you realised who I was."

"You a big disappointment to me," said Fizzy.

"Well if it's any consolation you are a disappointment to me also," I said, as I wiped away my make-up, "Remember that night we spent together?"

Fizzy did remember and seemed to go quite pale.

"I seem to have touched a nerve," I said.

Fizzy pushed the other artists preparing for their performance out and slammed the door. He then pointed his finger and told me never to speak to his daughter again.

"I haven't spoken to her for a while," I said. "I think she is quite capable of looking after herself anyway."

"Then what is all this Love Dungeon thing?" said Fizzy, pulling out a card and hurling it in my face.

I picked the card up and read it. It announced the services of the Love Dungeon.

"I don't know what this is at all," I said. "But it looks like I should. Thank you for drawing it to my attention."

"At first I think you still doing things with Alice," said Fizzy. "You two being English characters. I thought that was what the English did, but ..."

"You're right, it does not sound like your daughter's style."

"I found it in her room!"

"You should not have been looking."

"I been told she telephone these places, checking the rates."

"That's got nothing to do with me. I haven't seen her for two weeks. I've been very busy."

"I could have you disappear," said Fizzy, working himself up into a purple anger. "But she would never forgive me."

"I wouldn't be too pleased either."

"No you wouldn't."

"Well that's settled then. We separate. Go our own ways and that's the end of it."

Fizzy grabbed me by my false bosom, and stuck his face into mine.

"I trusted you," said Fizzy. "That is what annoys me."

Then he left and I quickly whipped off my frock and got back into civvies.

It had been fun for a while but I could see my period in Cop Show Heaven grinding to a halt and greater things beckoning. Except, I seemed to have become two separate characters. Perhaps that was inevitable. There would always be a part of me left behind.

CHAPTER SIX

I arrived at The Pig Out intending to irritate Cherry by fondling her buttocks at as many inappropriate moments as I could find. Instead, I found Alice and Padget gazing lovingly into each other's eyes over dinner.

I thought it might be rude not to join them, since I wanted to show that I had an emotional range that rose above jealousy. I felt that Padget, nervously twitching and playing with his ponytail, did not have such a range. He was very worried about the handover, since he was a dissident, so he kept telling me.

"We won't be staying on," said Alice. "There's plenty of work to be done at the San Francisco end."

"Ah, so you're not going to Hollywood."

"My writer lives in San Francisco."

"My writer lives there as well," said Padget. "And she intends to co-write with hers."

"I'm glad to hear that. And what of Lily?"

Padget grimaced and obviously did not like the sound of that word.

"She can come if she wants," said Alice.

"And if she stays, she stays with that father of hers? Do you really think that is wise?"

"It is of no concern of yours!" said Padget. "It is an internal family matter."

"Well of course I am not qualified to talk of such matters," I said, hating this man.

"No," said Alice. "It really isn't any of your business."

"Oh well," I said, "that's the end of it then. A shallower more pointless relationship I could never have hoped for. Goodbye."

Why I felt so annoyed, I could not say. Maybe I should not have felt anything at all, except that I did. Nevertheless, it was pointless. She was a mediocre piece of characterisation that had washed up in Cop Show Heaven and I was on my way to somewhere real. Why did I need to be worried about any of these mere traits? They were nothing.

I consoled myself with a trip to the disco. I arrived as the she-devils in their thongs and see-through dresses began to stomp to the sounds of the latest throbbing beat. It was good. The hormones that filled the air could not help but intoxicate. They

114

set me reeling from she-devil to she-devil, group to group, showing off my impeccable timing.

I was after flesh and anyone that had even the remotest sign of looking like Lily was fair game. I wanted such a girl. I needed such a girl. When I did find such a girl, it was Lily, the little devil.

"I thought you'd taken yourself off to a nunnery," I said.

"Why should I?"

I took her arm and pulled her off the dance floor to somewhere more conducive to conversation.

Lily squirmed at my hard grasp. I apologised and then tried to kiss her. She turned her head away.

"What on earth!" I said. "Don't you remember?"

"You don't tell me where you live and you don't remember my birthday ..."

"You could have phoned?"

"You haven't paid your bill!"

"Ah," I said. "Yes. I wondered why no-one was phoning me. I'll pay it and then we can talk."

"Why would I want to talk to you?"

Lily returned to her friends and made some comment that had them all staring and laughing at me. I contemplated returning to the dance floor and dragging her away but what did it matter? What did her opinion matter?

I slept unhappily alone in my new apartment that night. I could not help feeling that I should not be alone and that being alone made everything worthless. The constant rain added to my misery. When I woke, the handover had begun and I wanted to wallow in the pain of the angels drinking the entire day away. Then I would go with them to plague the new rulers. However, I had to go to work. It would be relatively easy. All I had to do was run through the crowds and keep in sight of the camera.

*

The moment of history arrived. All the celebrations looked like the sort of thing a well-meaning local Boy Scout Troop might put together if the weather and the leaky tent did not thwart them. Even so, I was a part of the proceedings.

115

Or at least the proceedings were to serve as a backdrop to what was the real business of the day, the creation of a fantasy that would for a few minutes be more real than anything else ... at least it was hoped it would become real.

The crowds were massing and the rain was falling. The police used their loudhailers to herd the crowd into one spot and then another. The crew and I found ourselves in no sight of the harbour.

"This will have to do," said Stirling, checking his watch.

As the fireworks burst in the air to fizzle in the downpour, I set to running from pursuers. One camera tried to keep with me as I barged through the crowd, an umbrella nearly skewering my eye. The cameraman caught my reaction. Good shot.

I ran on, and pushed into some children, separating them from their parents who yelled at me, as I pretended all hell was letting loose and guns were shooting at me.

The fireworks continued to flash and fizzle and crash. The Police moved to try to stop the surge I was causing. I leaped over a barrier and headed towards the electric light criss-crossed Dome of Copernicus and waded through the pond outside where plastic police cars lit from below flashed blue lights and screeched tyres, symbols of Cop Show Heaven, and endangered as a species. The police shouted and tooted their whistles. The camera crew backed off, leaving me splashing through to the other side of the pond without getting it on film. There would not be a second chance.

Stirling telephoned me and told me to try to make it to the front through the cathedral. They would then meet me under the flying buttresses outside. I ran through the building, dodging the leaflet stands and queues for the toilets, came out the other side with my heart pounding, and paused for breath in the steamy rain. Beside me, a man listened to the ceremony on his earplug radio.

"God's apparently weeping!" he said out loud to whoever passed by, and gave a strange laugh.

I gathered my breath and pushed through the crowd towards the buttresses. I could hear the wafting strains of orchestral tunes from the loudspeaker of the Stunt Museum where the final ceremony was to be held.

I stopped when I saw Stirling. I did not approach. Something was happening. There was a fight. There were shouts. There were the sounds of equipment being smashed. I hung back a little longer as the crowd panicked and tried to get away from the disturbance. Police were whistling. The fireworks came to their crescendo. A huge explosion brought cheers into the air, but little was seen but the steam caused as hot ashes hit the rain, which if anything grew fiercer tearing into the hanging pink and green paper bodies of the Nine Devils of Hades that lined the harbour front as decorations.

I managed to find my way to Stirling as he was being carried away, blood covering him from head to foot, a chop wound in his shoulder. The crew was searching the ground for a finger. The camera was smashed. Film had spewed out and unravelled among the crowd. Another crewman was on his phone to the other unit to see if they had seen anything. It seems they too had their story to tell, they had their wounds, their losses, and the shoot was at an end.

As the crowds began to leave the front, heading for their homes, soaked and steaming, umbrellas carried high, pick-pocketed and disgruntled as the party faded away, I went with the crew to recuperate and gather my thoughts. They found the restaurant had also been ransacked. Upon phoning the labs, they discovered the negatives of their previous rushes had been stolen in a break-in. This was a disaster. There would be no film now. The director's life was hanging on a thread. The film was stolen and it would take an awful lot of money to sort this out.

There was little to do but to head to The Pig Out where the party was beginning to get in gear. The count-down began when I arrived. "Ten ... nine ... eight," yelled the crowd packed so tight that water would not pass through. And the rain finally slowed to a drizzle. A man shook a red hat in front of my face and pointed out that God had signed it at the circus and it was worth fifteen thousand dollars now. The man was a toothless ex-con who had been in Cop Show Heaven for ten years and promised to stay on forever no matter who ran the place. He was a devil now, he proclaimed.

The young, the rich, the bankers in their pinstriped shirts and bowlers were on display. Everyone was flying the flag and when "three ... two ... one" came, the cheer went up and the flags

117

changed and a trumpeter played the opening call of Hell's Anthem, and everyone jeered. I was pushed one way and then another. I was not going anywhere and there was nowhere to go.

I squeezed inch by inch through the hormonal fug that would lead to many hangovers the next day and found myself in the cooler, emptier streets where an eerie silence had descended. Most people had homes to go to and had sat tight there as God sailed out of Cop Show Heaven on a cloud.

I walked to the legislative building. There a crowd of newspaper reporters and news crews gathered to watch the Democrats make their exit. Padgett was to give a speech from the balcony, a speech that was illegal now because no meeting of more than thirty was allowed.

The police stood by, their new badges in place, and watched and posed for photographs with pretty girls. Some people lit candles and I half expected to see Lily, but mostly the universal press were there to catch this last act of defiance ... or was it the start of the campaign for democracy in Hell as a whole? Would the devils rush in and stop this? It did not look like it. I could see the secret servicemen and the plain clothes men, the angels and the devils, circulating, phones in pockets, ear plugs in, noting who was there, looking out for guns, for trouble, for anything. I could hear a song being sung in the distance on a platform beneath the balcony. Every so often, someone shouted a slogan into the microphone and some people responded, but most of the press did not understand a word.

Cherry and Edward were trying to interview a couple of girls who were saying how they were there to support democracy.

"Why?"

"Because we like it."

"What benefits would it bring?"

"Freedom."

"Freedom from what?"

"Oppression."

"Whose oppression?"

"The Devil's."

"What if he won the election?"

"Then I guess that'd be OK."

Cherry noticed me watching her.

"You look terrible," she said.

I thought how terrible I felt and how empty. My portable phone began to ring. I had paid the bill, just in case someone important wanted to get in touch. I turned away from Cherry who was already busy trying to manoeuvre herself closer to Padgett. The strains of Beethoven's Fifth could be heard blasting out from somewhere in the distance. The acoustics were terrible and I could hear nothing of what was said.

I answered my phone and found Lily speaking. She was very excited. She wished I was there on the border to see the devils coming in with their white gloves and their armoured cars. Not that she could see much because it was raining hard. One landslide and the entire army would be washed away. She was going to cheer, but it was going to be an ironic cheer, she said.

"Goodbye," she said. "Sorry about your film. Fizzy is a horrible man. But you should have listened when he told you not to go with Stirling. He did warn you. He told me he did anyway and didn't want me to think he was getting at you. He can be very sensitive and very horrible. Goodbye. I suppose you won't be stopping much longer now. It was almost fun wasn't it?"

Then my battery ran out and her voice faded into the wind, the rain, and the boom of Beethoven and the little thin speech with its ripples of applause droned on and on. It was a moment of truth and the truth was, I was not a part of anything, I was not connected to anyone, I was a fiction that nobody read. How would Hollywood know of me now?

*

The rain continued to fall and I listened to its thump upon the top of the external part of the air-conditioner. This rattled and groaned and belched freezing air, failing to reduce the humidity, and since the rain had lowered temperatures to tolerable levels, was proceeding to freeze the toes that poked from my over-short bed.

The bedroom was sparsely furnished, as was the rest of the tiny fifteen foot by fifteen foot apartment, without drawers or cupboards, but merely a couple of chairs upon which I placed my suitcase. On the floor beside me was a radio, which burst into life with the morning news programme consisting initially of news of landslides and road floods, and then recaps of interviews with witnesses of the Devil's grand rain-drenched entrance into the newly constituted Cop Show Hell!

As I stirred from what I began to feel was an awful hangover and a numb sense of being frozen to death by a fridge freezer gone rampant, I began to remember the disaster of the previous day.

"Fucking bastard!" I muttered.

At least I was not missing any appendages unlike poor old Stirling. For some reason, that did not overly cheer me. Making a movie was hard work, both physically and emotionally, and when it was all for nothing, one felt like one's balls had been cut off.

"I'm in fucking hell!" I muttered. "And I am freezing to death!"

Then I seemed to go out of focus and only regain focus when I heard a grievance councillor on the radio taking phone-calls from various characters expressing their chagrin at God's having left them.

"I feel nothing for Hell," said one. "How am I supposed to respond to the Anthem when they play it in sports fields?"

If that was the guy's only problem, I thought, then I could hardly see the point of making the phone-call. After a few more calls of a similar nature saying how the angels were good guys and how the bastards had betrayed Cop Show Heaven and left, I could take no more and hit the radio snooze button. I had half a mind to phone the studio and tell everyone not to be so stupid.

For a while I mused about the nature of identity and what a wank it was to think about it. Then I shivered as lightening rent the sky, followed by my room plunging into darkness as yet more clouds wiped out what light there was, and more rain rolled down like a thundering waterfall. Crying under these circumstances seemed superfluous yet I felt like crying. I could hear a harp riffing as I was taken back years to my childhood...

There, through the soft-focus vaselined lens, I was staring out of the window at the cold northern hemisphere rains that confined me to the living-room of my parents' terrace house on all too many Sunday afternoons. My parents were snoring in armchairs. My brother was in his room sulking over his usual losing fight to put his stereo on at full blast, and I had nothing to do but pretend I was a malicious blob of rain marching down the pane to eat up all the other blobs. The crazy conversations I would have between one blob and another would no doubt fill a textbook of Freudian analysis.

I tried to recall what sort of thing I used to say, but to no avail. I suspect it was all plagiarised from Star Wars and the blob with the force would somehow overcome all other blobs until disappearing into the great stream of consciousness.

Sometimes these days could be warmly comforting, since the fire was blazing, and maybe my mother was singing to herself in the kitchen, and always my father was snoring, but mostly comfort was not what I felt. I felt a desire to scream. It seemed to me that these people were interested in nothing, had no life, at least none when I was around. They were like wardens in a prison, with their personalities, their homes, families, enthusiasms kept outside of the walls, to be put on as they took their uniforms off. So I wanted action, wanted the gabble of voices, of people, of places, of fantasy if nothing else was on offer.

Not a bad character profile for a hero really.

I had to get up then. If I were to avoid sinking back into the oblivion I had come to Cop Show Heaven to escape, I would have to get up and see people and try to get back on an even keel.

I dressed and stared out of the window. The road outside was knee deep in water and huge swirls of it were sweeping tree trunks, sewage, and cardboard boxes down a large storm-drain. It amused me to watch people with umbrellas wading across the road. Why they bothered with the umbrellas, I could not fathom. Maybe they symbolised something: lethal weaponry, high finance and formidable virgin nannies?

I could see no devils doing anything untoward, so I picked up my umbrella and drove the lift downstairs. Out on the street with my umbrella up, I relished the absurdity of bothering since the water swashed up to my knees.

I struggled upstream from the storm-drain and headed for the tram-stop where I hoped to catch one to meet up with Sydney. We would pour out our misery together.

At least I had a bit of money in the bank but ... and I shuddered at the outrageousness of Fizzy Tang! I would have to kill him. That was all there was for it. I would have to have my revenge upon the man.

"Don't be so stupid!" said Sydney, as he ushered me into his apartment.

Nevertheless, I was adamant. I wanted to know the names of which particular Triad group would be interested in catching Fizzy on his own.

"You could always go to the police?" ventured Sydney as he threw me a towel and gestured for his in-laws to turn the TV sound down. They looked up from their mah jong game. This was making such a clatter that I could hear little difference between when the TV was blaring and when it was not.

The children of the extended family were screaming in another room, zapping each other on some computer game while Sydney's number one wife busily hurried from one parent and uncle to the next offering tea-leaf-full refills for their lidded tea mugs.

"We're all waiting to go out to see the Devil's fireworks," explained Sydney as I failed to find anywhere to sit. "When the rain stops, the real festivities should begin, as opposed to God's cheapskate ones. Makes one feel abandoned doesn't it? When I saw God leave the harbour, there was a little lump in my throat."

"Bugger that," I said. "My director was being chopped up! They even stole the negatives of the film."

"There'll be another one," said Sydney. "You should take a philosophical viewpoint on this sort of thing."

"Oh yeah?" I said, failing to see how Sydney could be so calm considering how his secret arrangements with various Filipinas were about to hit the fan with an unwanted pregnancy. "I'll see how philosophical you get when your world crumbles."

"Nothing lasts," said Sydney. "It is all maya. That's Sanskrit for bollocks. I'm not sure I really believe in all that sort of stuff, but the Buddhists do have a point. Striving for one's ambitions could easily blind one to simple pleasures, and in the end, even when one achieves them, so what? You'll only be rewritten as a cockroach. Which is, as you would say, more bollocks. Far better to look at things from some sort of cosmic viewpoint where one appreciates the majesty of the infinite and the irrelevancy of much that we suffer so much angst over."

"And when your wife's chopping your bollocks off, I'd like to see you take a cosmic stance."

"Sssh!" said Sydney, ushering me to the door. "I think it must be time for you to leave right now. Try to calm down and do not do anything hasty."

Sydney slapped his hand over my mouth and gave me an angry stare.

"You were always a little shit," said Sydney. "And now you're fucked you want to fuck up everyone else."

"You're a phoney Sydney! A bullshit artist."

"It's ninety per cent of the game and you know it."

"That's what it was," I said. "I remember now. You were spouting something about mystical truths and then began laughing like a fat Buddha. Our writer was laughing and I could not see the joke. He was grinning like some idiotic cult member. It's all bollocks he said, and you said, *Precisely!* And you were gone and I was appearing on prime time TV as the devilishly handsome but tortured Detective Sergeant Dan Symonds. Then, when they revealed I was a transvestite, they shot me!"

"You have to make people want to believe," said Sydney, recalling fondly a gem of wisdom. "I think that was the only deep insight into the nature of things our man ever had."

"It's bollocks," I said.

"Precisely!"

"No, I don't mean that in any cosmic sense, I just mean it's bollocks!"

"But it almost made your career and I suspect it'll make it again."

"No," I said. "It fucked my career because our writer's a dickhead! He keeps wanting to add contradictions to our characters! But they're stupid contradictions. Me and you, STUPID! Me, great until I'm fucking about in an angora sweater! Doesn't the moron know, they want heroes to be straightforward! Give them a dead wife by all means, or a sick child to look after. Give them crippled legs to overcome, or some enigmatic inner torment that makes them obsess about justice! But you don't make them fucking juggling fairies or babbling sex maniacs who floss their intestines! Those are not popular heroes!"

"Whatever you think, Dan. Now piss off. There's a good chap."

"You're quite satisfied that our creator is a sick man and we stand absolutely no chance of becoming much-loved literary characters?"

"If I did, I'd be a different person. I accept. You don't. That's where we go our separate ways."

Sydney pushed me out into the hall and closed the security gate, then the door, leaving me wondering why I came in the first place. Indeed, why was I arguing with Sydney at all? It was not his fault. If anyone should be angry with anyone, it should be him angry with me. I at least existed for a moment, whereas he lingers amongst the early drafts, forever deleted.

The rain kept on coming down. Thousands upon thousands of millimetres of rain fell upon Hell and I could not imagine how this process continued. Somewhere the ice caps were melting and steaming up the atmosphere and here I was waiting to drown in a mad rush to a taxi.

I stood in the entrance of the flats with a group of others determined to make their way through the streets. They were all fascinated by the ability of the rain to fall in the kind of sheets that even the most apocalyptic scene in the last three quarters of a movie could not contain with any degree of credibility. I felt a wave of depression. I should have been a character in *Breakfast at Tiffany's* where the no-name cat, hurled out into the rain by Holly Golightly had to be rescued as a symbol of commitment, of recognition of the real self, and of something I never was quite clear about…

My life was not a film though, at least not yet, and instead I ran from shop front to shop front until I arrived, dripping, at Yeltsin's Bar. There it was guaranteed that a bunch of Angels would be holed up in the dark, knocking back the beers and nursing hangovers from the night before.

I sank into a pint and listened to the jokes about the ceremony: the silly uniforms of the devils, the pasty-faced smiling masks our leaders wore, the stiff handshakes, the tears in God's eyes and the rain dripping.

I kept thinking I could have any of these angels, sitting about in their grubby T-shirts, lighting up their cigarettes. They had trekked across the Great Divide, they had seen the sights in

Heaven, fought with border guards in Hell, and got stoned on the Great Road to Inspiration. Nothing could faze them, but I thought I could faze them all right. I could make my move and show them something they would never forget.

"And who are you going to be?" they asked, their hair greasily flying in all directions as they stubbed cigarettes into spilt beer. I had been grinning and laughing at their jokes about the cock-ups of the fireworks and how *The Devil Daily* had already put out an eye-witness account of today's sunny festivities, before the government cancelled them because of the rain.

"Guess," I said.

"A Merchant Banker..."

This caused catcalls.

"And if you're not a banker," they continued, "Then you'll be cast as a spy!"

"I would have been out of here on the boat by now," I said.

"Then you'll be a layabout like the rest of us."

Moments like this were supposed to give one moments of clarification. One's goals were supposed to be simplified. Wisdom was supposed to come out of disaster. However, all that kept coming into my mind was how I could pass the time fucking someone, or sneaking up behind Fizzy and smashing his brains out.

My mobile telephone rang like a warning from hell. It was Fizzy sounding very apologetic about what had happened.

"It had to be done Dan," he said. "It was unfortunate that you were involved, but I did warn you."

"Uhuh?" I said.

"Don't be mad at me. I'll make it up to you."

"Why should you?"

"Because I like you, Dan, and you can do me a favour."

"I'm sick of doing you favours. When are you going to do me one?"

"I will! I will. You got to trust me."

"Uhuh?"

"That's right. Look. Can you check out how Alice is doing? I think she going to leave and I want to be up to date on what is happening."

"Why? I haven't noticed you and your daughter pining over each other. I don't get your game."

"Just do it. Just have a look in. See what the score is."

"Have you ever thought of talking to her yourself?"

"She never tells me anything."

I hung up. In the meantime, an Angel had moved in closer and was talking about the microwave radiation cellular phones emitted, and how they were frying people's brain cells.

"Excuse me," I said. "I must make a call."

"What?" Lily answered

"It is I. And I am in love with you."

"Are you drunk?"

"Probably, though I am not making much of an effort in that direction. You see, with all this rain, you're my no-name cat. Understand?"

"What?"

"You're right. That's a bad analogy."

"You are drunk. Talk to me when you're sober."

"I will."

The phone went dead.

The rain had abated and left the street outside humid but fresh. The diesel fumes of the mini-buses had been washed out of the air and instead there was a hint of jasmine, of greenery and earth from the hundreds of potted plants that dangled precariously from overhead balconies. I made my way to the hospital to see how Stirling was doing.

*

"Not so good," croaked Stirling, as I sat beside him in his private hospital room. The décor was minimalist: whitish paint and nothing else, and a very high bed that I thought must be designed to kill any who were irritating enough to attempt sleep walking. It probably made life easier for the nurses.

It did not take long to realise that Stirling was not easy to visit in hospital. There was little we had in common other than the film and that seemed a sore point.

"The bastard wants me to pay a ransom for the negatives."

"Oh well, not everything is lost."

Stirling held up his hand with the missing index finger.

"If I go to the police," said Stirling, "he burns the lot."

"Go to the police after you get it back."

"Oh yeah? This town's gone to Hell! How d'you think I'm going to get out of here if I do that?"

"You'll have to pay him then won't you?"

"I won't give him the satisfaction. The film stinks."

"You were very pleased with the rushes."

"That's what I always say. And who cares about Cop Show Heaven now? Its moment has passed."

"But you were so keen ..."

"If only the devils had marched in and slaughtered a few thousand, then the whole enterprise would have been worth it."

"Well then, you get well and get that film and er, if you need me for some retakes ..."

"Yeah yeah," said Stirling, grimacing as he tried to ease his shoulder into a more comfortable position. "Just half an inch and they would have had my jugular. These guys have no imagination. They have not got a clue."

"Right," I said backing out of the room.

In the corridor I met Josephine, who was walking about in her dressing gown, looking for Stirling's room.

"You're in here as well are you?"

"Yes, I'm dying, Dan. The heroin they give me is good, but my leg is not good and if the surgeons start chopping they have to chop off everything. Legs. Arms. Maybe I should call on Fizzy. He is very good at that."

This should have put my own predicament into some sort of perspective. Much to my shame, it did not. I'm shallow. I'm written that way.

"You should learn to empathise a bit more, Dan. You'll get more parts then."

I leaned forward and kissed her on the lips. I pretended that she did not smell of hospital soap or that she was suspiciously a man. What did it matter? She would never tell anyone and soon she would be swimming with all the other turtles in the pond, in the next circle of Hell.

"I like the beard," said Josephine. "It gives you a warmer, maturer look. Keep it and see what happens."

I walked away feeling the half-inch of stubble I had.

*

127

For the next few days, I brooded about what to do about Fizzy. I concluded, several times, that I would either kill him or see if I could at least get him to give me some part in a movie.

When not brooding, I managed a phone conversation with Lily. She had been spending her time handing out leaflets for a hunger strike against the cancelling of all last-minute legislation passed by God. Thus, she was busy with the struggling masses, and most likely no-name cats as well. But she was also busy reconciling with her father, which was definitely a sign in my eyes that she was not perfect.

I was not so sure I loved this rather earnest young girl. Perhaps everything had changed and the rules were different. I had a beard for instance. It was a pointy sort of beard, with sideburns that I shaved into a diabolic triangle. I thought it gave me a devilish sort of look. Marginal notes in the writer's exercise book were beginning to amount to something.

I bumped into Alice in the shopping mall and she was going to Heaven's new Embassy for her passport renewal. Padget was going to meet her at some posy wine bar, so I decided to keep him company while she concluded her business.

Padget, on finding me in the restaurant was not very friendly. I kept saying that I did not want to disturb his lunch, but I obviously did.

Padget fidgeted with his long unstylish ponytail hanging over the front of his shoulder, and sat glumly watching me tuck into garlic bread.

"Wasn't there some rude poem of yours calling the Devil a bad egg or something?"

"God just laughed at me when I told him why I needed asylum. Bastard!"

"And then the Devil didn't beat down your door and cart you off?"

"You never know when he'll come," said Padget mournfully. "Maybe he thinks it's a better torture letting me think he'll come."

"Did he send you threatening letters?"

"He is pretending to ignore me."

"I see," I said. "I can empathise very sincerely with that. What does Alice think about this mental torture that the Devil is putting you through?"

"We're going to get married," said Padget, his eyes suddenly scanning the menu. "I don't like this place. Too much cheese."

"You'll have to tell Alice about the cheese if you marry her," I said, rubbing as much garlic butter into my beard as I could. I thought a character like me would smell of garlic. "I bet up North in the gulags they feed nothing but cheese to the prisoners."

Padget glanced up from his menu. Our eyes met.

"Is there something wrong with you?" said Padget.

"No. Nothing could be finer," I said.

"You have a strange look in your eye."

"No I don't," I said.

"I heard they stopped you filming."

"Who stopped us?"

"Most likely on orders from Hell," said Padget. "See what I mean?"

"I doubt it."

"You were making anti-Devil propaganda," said Padget. "So Fizzy most likely did someone a favour by hacking up Stirling. That way he could continue to operate after the handover."

"I didn't notice anything particularly anti-anything in Stirling's movie."

"There's that strange look in your eye. Are you sure you are feeling alright?"

I felt I was feeling all right.

"Perhaps you're in shock," said Padget. "Reality has suddenly hit you."

Padget could be very irritating.

"So you're getting married then," I said, changing the subject. "And what about Lily? Is she full of approval now?"

"She's going to come with us but I don't think that is a good idea," said Padget, pulling a face. "Step-fathers are never liked."

"Especially ones that tried to fuck step-daughters."

Knives, forks, plates and glasses crashed and shattered as Padget lunged across the table at me.

There was a hush in the restaurant as Padget gathered his dignity and picked up the pieces of glass with the help of a waiter.

Alice arrived and found him on his knees.

"Just a little accident," I said, mopping up the wine spilt down my shirt. "Padget had a bit of a turn. But I forgive him. I guess it's all the stress he's been under recently."

*

"That's right," I said, as I rode beside Fizzy in his van.

"I knew it!" said Fizzy. "But she hates him."

"Obviously she does not hate him that much," I said. "He is a handsome sort of chap. A little nervy and prone to jealousy, mind, but he did get Alice that job as interesting mixed-race married couple. I think Home Box Office are casting them right now."

"She'll screw anyone for a fucking job."

"What sort of job was she after with me?"

"Whore!"

"I thought so," I said, stroking my beard.

There was an impishness to my character, I decided, a sort of Machiavellian, King John, Sheriff of Nottingham sort of devilishness. Any minute now I would be bursting into song and juggling something. No wonder I was doomed.

Fizzy drove to his favourite pick-up point and transferred several devils who were waiting in the lichee orchard into the back of the van. I was riding shotgun again, this time with my passport at the ready to flash at the police.

"It's all legal," explained Fizzy. "Legal illegals. The Cop Show Hell law says if you got Cop Show parent then you are citizens, only you weren't before the Devil made the law so you couldn't come in."

I didn't understand what he meant, but I could not be bothered to get it clarified.

"Then you're paying me for nothing," I said, which seemed to be the reasonable conclusion.

"Ah, but we think we better keep them hidden because they might still send them back."

"So long as I get my money," I said, feeling Rhett Butlerish, "I don't give a damn."

"That's the way with all immigrants," said Fizzy. "They learn too soon that money is all that counts and that repressive governments don't stop you earning it, they just stop you earning it legally. But illegal money is always a lot more."

Fizzy laughed and drove round potholes and landslides and through floods and roadblocks manned by police who did not bother to stop us.

"I hear you've scored a few points with the new masters?" I said.

"What do you mean?"

"Stirling was seen as a worthy target."

"If that's what people want to believe, let them."

"I'll tell people that it was just business then."

"I don't like that beard of yours, Dan."

"It makes me look disreputable doesn't it?"

"Why you want to go round looking like that?"

"I go round with you don't I?"

I grinned and could tell that Fizzy disliked my grin.

"Whatever you've got," I said, "I want to be a part of it."

A week later, which I spent growing my beard and pensively reading Bakunin in the public library, Fizzy took me for a midnight ride on his speedboat ...

Bakunin? Oh, I don't know why! It just said so in the script! I personally have not got a clue who he was. Some Russian I think. Anarchist. He had a similar beard.

Where was I? In the speedboat ...

There was no chance of using this for smuggling runs, at least not nowadays. Those required big six-engined affairs with a huge capacity for lots of contraband. This boat was for checking on the fishing-boats that brought in the illegal devils. An easy few thousand dollars was to be earned running a few people ashore and setting them up with part time contracts labouring.

Every week Fizzy did a tour of the islands to check that none of the people on his pay-roll were doing something stupid like camping on the water's edge where police patrols could see them. He thought that I would be excellent for this duty, being a cop show character and thus beyond suspicion. So he took me for a ride to show me the ropes and introduce me to a few of the people I would have to deal with.

None of these characters spoke English and they all looked upon me with deep suspicion but Fizzy smoothed the way and I played the part.

"This is all excellent research for that role you are going to give me in the next film you do," I said.

"Yeah the next film," said Fizzy. "But there's a bit of a slump on at the moment. And Josephine's dead now so there might be a longer wait for another job."

"I'm sorry to hear that," I said, genuinely feeling that I should have gone to visit her in the last few days of her life. "Was she a man by any chance?"

"Maybe she was."

"She had a deep voice. And a fat cock in her pants."

"How do you know?"

"She got very close to me once."

"Oh well, she dead and burning in Hell now. We'll never know for sure."

I tried a little sympathy then and could not find any. In fact, I found myself feeling rather clear of emotions and confusions. Maybe that is what you felt when you were doomed to stay in Cop Show Hell forever.

So I took up Fizzy's job offer and met bunches of his skinny little devils as they huddled in muddy clearings in the hills. As individuals they were of as much interest as Josephine and her death. I could have blown them away easily with a pump action shot gun if they turned bad on me.

"If they get sick," said Fizzy, "don't fack about with medicine. Get them on the boat back home. Then if they die, over the side they go. Right?"

"If you say so, boss," I said.

"You've the right attitude," said Fizzy, "You know that?"

"It couldn't be better."

*

Lily heard about my activities. She phoned me up and berated me every time she heard how I had been doing some business for her father.

"If you're so righteous, then report him to the police."

132

"I don't agree with the immigration policy here," she said. "And he is my father after all."

I was beginning to hate Lily. I had risked my neck for her. I had braved police roadblocks. I had befriended cutthroats and con-artists. I had traipsed through jungles, tripping once over a pangolin that was burrowing through the undergrowth at my feet. I had sweated through the bamboo groves; braved landslide and flood to take pay packets to my teams of illegally employed devils ...

This pleasure in adventure I eulogised in my diary and long battery-killing phone-calls to Lily. All this, I told her, was for her. And she was not pleased.

"You are reconciling yourself with the man," I said. "So why should I not do likewise?"

"I am but I don't think it is right," said Lily, who had returned to school because, as she said, "Education is necessary and I must educate my teachers."

The school's raising of Hell at the morning assembly had been a traumatic experience for Lily.

"Head for California then!" I said.

But for Lily, the anger, the annoyance, the bitter twists and distortions of her character profile made her want to infiltrate Hell even further.

"Come and meet me then," I said.

Unbelievably, we went for an ice-cream. She was from a completely different genre to me. She was shopping-malls and soda-fountains whereas I ...

"My life is an adventure straight out of a Conrad novel," I told her, as I stroked my beard. "I slip off into the hills, into the bays, and into the underworld. It's marvellous."

Lily ate her sundae and told me that she was not sure my beard was a good idea and that I seemed to have given up all my ambitions to be an heroic character.

"I am a villain," I said. "My writer has decided that since nobody empathised with me when I was good, then I might as well be bad."

"That's what I thought," said Lily. "But my father is going to get you into trouble."

"And then will you save me?"

"No way!" she said. "You're beyond saving."

133

I stared into her eyes until she blushed. I could not work out whether I felt anything for her. Her attractiveness was not a rarity, and one might say that the blue eyes amidst the black hair were more a distraction than an enhancement.

"So have you been writing pornographic e-mails to anyone lately?"

"No!" said Lily. "We don't do that stupid thing anymore. There are more important things to do."

"Oh?"

"Oh yes," said Lily. "Who knows what secret deals there were and what really is going to happen! Will the courts be able to challenge the legislation? Can it challenge anything that the Devil wants, and can it succeed? These are very important."

"More important than us?"

Lily blushed again and looked down. In her world it was marriage and diamonds forever. In mine, it was ass-meat and sticky nasty facials. I could feel myself slipping once again outside of the mainstream.

"We have to make sacrifices for a stable society," she said.

"Fuck that."

"I don't like that beard," said Lily. "It makes you look a little mad. And it makes you sound a little bitter."

I stood up and took hold of Lily's hand.

"Come on. The flat's not much to look at but we can be alone together. You are sixteen aren't you?"

In the taxi on the way, Lily told me that she found it odd to be with a man who had slept with her mother and her father.

She was not impressed when I led her to my apartment. It was grey sheets and peeling wallpaper and she was fresh linen and rose petals. I could only imagine that she was there because of some perverse literary game.

"It won't be mine for much longer," I said, by way of explaining the lack of furniture. "But there's a good view."

Lily turned her back on the tiny room and stared out of the window at the rain.

"When I was a boy," I said, placing myself squarely behind her, "I used to see the rain on the window as a battleground."

"There's been something like 1,200 millimetres of rain over the territory in the past month. It's a one hundred and fifty year record."

"Is that so? How fascinating."

I kissed the back of her neck. The smell of her skin, the smoothness, the way youth radiated out of it, sent shivers through me.

"Stop it!" said Lily. "I've seen where you live. Now I should go."

This was one of those situations in which I felt no judge would ever convict me: a young girl goes back to an apartment with a villainous looking man in the middle of the afternoon and then says she never suspected that there was any sexual intention. A likely story they would say. If she cried rape then it would merely be that she changed her mind after the event. As every old judge knows, if a man ever took notice of the protestations of every young woman, no-one would ever get laid at all! Especially not fat old judges.

"No I don't think we should," said Lily, but she was flat on her back without any screaming and struggling.

My hand expertly slid up her skirt and within seconds I had her squirming and panting as I went through the numbers, pressing the right buttons, massaging the right spot, surprising and teasing each erogenous zone in their recommended sequence. I swear my fingers vibrated.

Afterwards she lay in my arms cooing and purring as the sweat dripped off us. All I kept thinking was how I should have put the air-conditioner on and how I had now had my revenge on Fizzy and how momentary the pleasure had been.

"I love you," whispered Lily. "I've never felt anything like this before. I don't know how I'm going to get through the day feeling this. I can't concentrate on anything else ..."

And she was off again, this time trying to put into practice what she had read somewhere, what she had just learnt, and no doubt a few other things she had fantasised about in her e-mails to complete strangers. Nevertheless, it did not matter what she was doing because she was glowing and sweat was spouting out of every pore as if her whole body was in the throes of an orgasm. And maybe it was. I found it a big turn-on and lay back as she squirmed, squealed and writhed on top of me, as light as a feather, but so firm. This was beginning to develop into the sort of narrative in which inserting a live goldfish into a virginal vagina began to make marketing sense. One could feel the disrespect for the general public's intelligence and taste reaping the lucrative rewards for all involved in the process. I could feel all the necessary popular ingredients for access to the psyche of the un-imagined accruing to me.

The question was, did I love her or did I not give a toss? I didn't know.

Finally, Lily was exhausted and unable to do more than sleep and I cooled myself beside the window watching the rain. How could I feel so bad for making her so ecstatically happy?

When Lily woke up I was full of the decision I had made.

"I'm going to give up attempting to be a believable character," I told her. "It is leading nowhere. I'm going to marry you and you can go to university while I work."

"Doing what?" she said incredulously from behind the steam of the shower she now took.

"Doing unbelievable things! I could perform for the visiting angels in the hotels."

"What about Hollywood?"

"It's not happening is it? The breaks aren't coming."

"My father saw to that," said Lily leaving the shower and looking so fresh and pink that I just had to fuck her again. I even managed to juggle a few beer mats at the same time.

"Do me," she panted, opening her mouth expectantly.

I almost called in Sydney to help me complete the scenario. Where sex was concerned people would rather deal with the fantasy than the reality.

*

Fizzy then promised me there would be a part in the new Kung Fu movie he was working on. I would be the badly acted, badly written, Westerner that everyone beats up in a Chinese movie. As repayment for his consideration I offered him some advice on how to get in Lily's good books.

"What you ought to do about Lily is impress her somehow," I said. "Show her whose side you are on. Then she might listen to you. What you need, is a nice dissident to smuggle in."

"Why's that?"

136

"Lily will think you are her hero and everyone will be happy about your daughter staying on without her mother's supervision."

"Don't think there's much supervision there at the moment."

"But even so," I said, "everyone would much rather you be a hero than a cheap opportunist exploiting the masses for all they are worth."

"Fack orf," said Fizzy, "You don't know the half of it!"

Back at the studios I relaxed in the office as Fizzy presented some Polaroids to the production assistant. Dennis, the English director, walked in with a script under his arm. He had suffered an outrageous delay in finishing his advert. He needed one last golden sunshine shot but rain and more rain had made him despair that it would ever happen.

In the meantime, though, he had been working on his writer, briefing her about various interesting action stories that might make an independent movie and he liked my beard. He threw his script at me and told me to let him know what I thought.

This turn up was a little worrying because half the turtles in Hell used to be characters in an unmade independent movie and it looked as if I was heading that way.

*

"Padget's character is a political researcher in Washington," bragged Alice.

I knocked back another gin at the bar of The Pig Out. I hated to think that someone could think Alice was a more interesting character than me.

"Very nice. And you? How have you been re-written?"

"I'm a columnist."

"Well that's a big change."

"Cynic," said Alice. "You want to get out of town for a while. You should find a beach and some girls. That should make you more interesting. You know, if nobody is interested in you, they will stop trying to write you and then you won't exist at all."

"Maybe when the rain stops, we should all go on a picnic," I suggested, wondering how on earth that would make me in the least bit more interesting!

"Who's we?" said Alice.

"Everyone. A sort of farewell reconciliation for the sake of Lily, if no-one else."

*

By now, I had found myself another apartment. One of Fizzy's friends wanted a flat-sitter to protect the furnishings from theft. So, I was privileged to have furniture this time. The view was not a bad one either. I could make out the harbour through the gaps between the buildings. The downside was that eventually someone that Fizzy knew was bound to notice Lily's comings and goings.

When she arrived, we kissed, had some tea and then looked at our watches and said things like, "Shall we start?" Sometimes we did not start, but sat around eating pizza, watching rented videos and talking about when we should announce our engagement, or if we should.

I could tell my writer was in trouble again. I had got the girl and there was no end in sight, no happy ever after. This was messy and if I was ever to return to the consciousness of the real world, I would have to conform to the conventions of story-telling.

"Maybe we should appear in public with your parents," I suggested. "We could then pretend that our being together started up then, and gain their blessing."

"The end."

"That's right. The End! And we're whole again."

"You mean, we're turtles!"

It was apparent that there was a very thin line between being irritating, interesting and so boring that you drop out of the realms of fiction into the pit of burnt-out personalities that eke out a meagre existence floating in murky water and fighting for a bit of rock to stand on for a touch of sunlight. Time was running out. The third act had to kick into gear and somehow, I had to find the tiny element of nobility that would transfigure me. But what could I possibly do? I had to become a character who schemed instead of one who merely reacted.

*

138

The rain had stopped for a weekend, long enough for my plan to be put into action. The sediment that was washed into the surrounding seas settled and instead of the muddy colour, a blue returned. Palm trees, golden sands, noisy excited cicadas rattled constantly in the heat-haze of the jungles. It was the perfect setting for an adventure film.

Padget rubbed oil into Alice's back. Lily splashed about the water in what her mother called the most obscene bikini she had ever seen. And I was there as Uncle Dan.

We were on an unnamed island. Fizzy had driven us here then sped off in the boat to pick up a few forgotten beers. This was to be a going-away party.

On a day like today I could see myself staying forever, unless the sharks that habitually chewed the legs off unsuspecting swimmers every year managed to get me stuck in their teeth.

So here I was on the beach and the sun was blazing. No talk of mini-ice-ages, merely ozone depletion and pollution. And land-slips. There were several red scars in the hills from where rain had washed down the topsoil and a few hundred illegal immigrants had been buried.

Any minute now, I thought, there would be a whiff of diesel and a long snakehead would swing round in the ocean, spraying water up onto the beach. Then another would come into view and the rattle of small arms would accompany a series of fountains that would have Lily rushing for cover and Alice and Padget leaping up and ridiculously walking forward to take a look. I would shout at them to get away from the water's edge.

It would be a simple sort of scam. Fizzy would turn up with a couple of dissidents and usher them into the hills. I would then explain that they would hide out until a freighter could be found to take them to Heaven, where they would apply for asylum because they were real dissidents, unlike phoney old Padgett! This would establish Fizzy as one of the good guys and not a mere gangster and Lily would plead to stay with him, and Alice would be less convinced of my inherent evil.

In return for reconciling Fizzy with Lily, I would be offered her hand and everyone would be friendly and live happily ever after.

There was another scenario though, where I exposed the fraud and got my revenge upon Fizzy. Then I would reveal, as a coup de grace: the obscenities that I had been using his daughter for.

I could sense the pain of my writer, throwing page after page away. At each throw I could sense the turtles in the pond outside the Cop Show Heaven Studios shifting over a little to make some room.

Then Fizzy turned up grinning from ear to ear as he leapt out of the motorboat, clutching a crate of champagne and a sack of melting ice.

"What is all this about!" demanded Alice.

"I'm going into film production," Fizzy announced. "So I thought now was a good time to announce it. Strictly legitimate of course."

"God help us," cried Padget.

Fizzy uncorked a hot bottle of champagne loosing most of it by spraying the contents over everyone, sending them screaming in all directions. Fizzy could not work out why they all thought this was a dismal sort of act.

"I thought everyone would be pleased I'm going to make more movies," said Fizzy, pouring himself another glass of champagne.

When the BBQ blazed, Fizzy and Padget fought over how long a fish ball took to cook and whether blackening them with soot was carcinogenic or not.

"He's barmy," said Lily. "Completely off his rocker."

I lay claim to a smoking sweet potato.

"When you going to give Stirling his film back?"

"When I've finished it for him," said Fizzy. "I checked it out. It's crap. You wouldn't want to be a part of that. But now, with a few decent chases and some real action, it could amount to something."

"You're *reshooting* it?"

"Only the bits he couldn't finish. We did a deal. Since he didn't use my services when he should, and has now seen the error of his ways, I get credited as second unit director and associate producer. Not bad eh?"

"And his finger?"

"What about his finger?"

"He doesn't mind that you chopped it off?"

"No," said Fizzy. "He understands business."

I bit my way through the hot skin of my potato. With a temperature of thirty-three degrees centigrade and ninety-five percent humidity, a good hot potato and lots of alcohol was just what I needed.

Alice now started accusing Fizzy of being without scruples and caring nothing for anyone and Padget started accusing Lily of being secretive, brazen, and dishonest with her mother. And Lily accused them all of being heartless and not loving the motherland, despite what her father claimed he was doing.

I kept out of the bickering. I saw it as a family thing and almost felt sorry for Fizzy. He denied his indifference to the suffering of mankind and started to defend his case by talking about why he worked so hard. He was doing it so Lily and Alice could live in expensive apartments, wear expensive clothes and enjoy expensive restaurants.

The day was not an entire success or disaster, but then whatever was? I managed not to spill the beans about Lily and me although I thought Lily might have wanted me to. However, since there was already an argument going on, it seemed best not to add to it. Besides, I was going to get my film finished, or at least Fizzy was going to.

The boat-ride back to the bus terminal was as hair-raising as one might expect with a stuntman driver, and the silence among all parties made it all the more terrifying.

That night, as I dreamt of turtles crawling in the mud, slithering over each other's backs to catch a glimpse of the sun, a blinding flash of light almost knocked me out of my lonely bed. That is, there was a loud crack of thunder, a huge fizzing flash of lightening, and sparks shot out of the electric plugs about the walls. I found myself on the floor gasping for breath and wondering if I had been struck by lightening, or enlightenment. Since I was alive and did not have a gaping smoking hole where my head was, I assumed the latter.

*

I awoke feeling so pure that mere mortals would find me transparent. The moral centre of my humanity had been touched.

"Bollocks," I said. "It is bollocks isn't it?"

The taxi-driver adjusted his rear-view mirror and gave me a quick once over.

"Maybe you get too much sun?"

"Ah, it is that I am in the sun too much," I said, touching my peeling red face and recalling Shakespeare's Hamlet. *You could lay bets that he was not to be found hanging about the bars of Cop Show Hell!*

I doubt that the taxi-driver had a clue what I was talking about, but I wondered if there was something in my thought processes. One's brain could be fried by all sorts of things, after all, authority and sunlight being part of the same package.

"But being human," I philosophised, "and sensing all the connotations of that word, being open and aware to potential and weakness, and the dark and the light side, and accepting it …"

"What?"

I tried to collect my thoughts into a more succinct package.

"I ..."

"You just have to learn to understand how others are feeling," said the taxi-driver, explaining my own thoughts to me.

"Exactly!" I said. "Empathy!"

"Much better than that."

"Well ... er ... sympathy?"

"Too sentimental."

"Well whatever."

"Whatever it is, you gotta get it."

"That's right. But how will I know when I have it?"

"You won't but others will."

"And so what do I do?"

"You do what you have to do."

"Precisely. And ... and what's that?"

"You bask in the sun and keep your head in your shell."

CHAPTER SEVEN

"I have these extraordinary conversations with this taxi-driver who has the most extraordinary haircut," I said when I met Alice for lunch. She had taken over from the absent Sydney. I suspected that he was scattered about the rubbish dumps in several different black plastic dustbin liners or at least in hiding in the jungles from his enraged wife.

Alice picked over her salad.

"When are you going to leave?" I said. "Not that I want you to leave. But I'd hate Lily to be around when the shit hits the fan."

"What shit?"

"Er, well," I said, "we're sort of having an affair at the moment and when she leaves with you, well…"

There, I admitted it. I told her. Now what was I supposed to do? And why had I told her? Because I felt pure. I wanted everything out in the open. I wanted my moral centre firmly established. I wanted loose ends to be tied up and I wanted to be free of Lily. End of story. Otherwise I'd turn into Sydney, Lily would be a little foreign wife, and we would be stuck in Hell, forever bit-part players in half-baked scenarios.

The inspiration that had struck me was that, whatever I did, I had to avoid settling for Hell's endless insubstantiality. I had to set the plot rolling again or else I would be going nowhere.

Alice recovered from a coughing fit and asked me to repeat what I said just in case she had not heard me right.

"Fizzy should never get to know this, so I'm telling you so that you can stop Lily from doing anything she would regret. You see, she had this crush on me. And, well, with my own apartment and lots of opportunity, we sort of got together. One thing led to another and I am sorry, but I thought I loved her. I do, but I don't think a sixteen-year-old is really someone I should be having a torrid affair …"

"Torrid?"

"Wrong word …"

It did not matter what I said after that. Alice tipped her plate over me and stabbed her fork into my nose. I was thankful that she missed skewering my eye but I fell backwards into the waiters, wine buckets and buffet tables and found the same

143

waiter picking up the broken glass that picked it up the last time I provoked an argument in the place.

The next thing I heard was the click of a taxi door. Then I fell into the back seat as it roared me away to safety.

"This empathy game," I muttered, "is not so easy is it?"

"If that is what you are playing."

"And if it isn't?"

"Then it is even harder."

"What is?"

"Whatever you are thinking."

"How the hell do I know what to think? I'm waiting for an inspired writer!"

"No," said the taxi-driver. "You should try to be what is best. From that basis everything else will grow and be for the best. Your job is to be. You have to take responsibility for that otherwise there would be no Cop Show Heaven, just the waste paper bin."

"You're a post modernist aren't you?"

"Neo-post-modernist. I only believe in designer labels."

"And morality?"

"Consensual codes of conduct."

"And can I be happy within this context?"

"You cannot have happiness without sadness."

"I'm sad now."

"No, you're pathetic now."

"I should have lied?"

"That all depends what you are lying about."

"The truth."

"That concept is very unreliable at the best of times, especially within a fictional construct."

"What the fuck then, does it take to get out of this place?"

"Wisdom."

"What the fuck is that?"

"One of the signs of wisdom is not getting angry with taxi-drivers, especially those who may or may not exist except as figments of the mind of a fictional character projecting his own thoughts onto the back of bad haircut."

"And what if I do become angry with you?"

"Then you become a turtle."

"You have an answer for everything don't you?"

"But not necessarily the correct answer. Of course, you don't necessarily have the correct question."

"So between my inane questions and your incorrect answers, where does that leave me?"

"I mentioned the turtles, didn't I?"

*

"What on earth happened to your nose?" asked Dennis, the English director.

More food was being consumed. Dennis had asked me to lunch. He was on his way home the next day, and wanted a last word about his project.

"The nose," he continued, "looks awful. The beard I like. The nose, nada!"

"I had a fork inserted," I explained. "But I decided it didn't suit so had it removed. The scar, so I'm told, will heal. But the mental scars probably won't."

"Well I guess it could have been worse. I hear they chop your dicks off here."

"They also stick them on as well."

"Unreal," he said. "So what did you think of my man's script?"

I could not remember him giving me a script. Maybe he did, maybe he did not. Either way, I did not know anything about it.

"I thought it was OK," I lied.

"We'll rewrite it. Don't you worry. But ... you're the sort of character who makes this all so easy! My writer used to work on your old show. She loved the actor who played you, in more ways than one. He rogered her raw!"

"No doubt under my influence."

"Exactly. So it was a real piece of luck bumping into you out here. This is going to happen! I love it when it does that."

I suppose scripts in Cop Show Heaven ... now Hell ... are the scripts that writers throw away. I assume that's why they are full of convoluted plots fed by coincidences. This, by the way, seemed the typical *deus ex machina* that often resolved an episode of *West End Central*. Some last minute confession or some piece of hearsay from the sub-plot would always inspire the hero to try just one last thing. Providing things moved fast

145

enough at the end, nobody noticed, or cared to notice the absurdity.

I decided it did not matter whether I had read the script or not. It would not be the one anyone ended up shooting anyway, so whatever it was ...

"It deserves to be made. It is probably one of the finest scripts I've read for a long time."

"It's not bad is it? At least, it is very doable. And that is what counts. It is very of the moment."

"She's screwing the producer is she?"

"If you've got it, you might as well use it."

"She should go far."

*

I, in beard and uniform, my face pummelled and bloodied, screamed "Eat Death, Yellow Devils", and fired off a burst of flame-thrower that sent some of Hell's finest stuntmen leaping from a jeep covered in flames. The jeep careered toward me and I looked at it in terror. There is a pyrotechnical explosion as the jeep knocks me clear, though not obviously clear in the smoke and noise ...

"The bullets inside me are so hot, but why do I feel so cold?" I said, very unclear as to my meaning, which is nothing new.

There was another thing that was unclear: why was I in combat uniform and where had I obtained the flame-thrower?

Things were moving too fast in the re-shooting of Stirling's movie for me to have time to try to figure out where this extra material was supposed to be in the context of the story. Somehow I was fighting off the invading hordes of devil renegades who were determined to make the handover a bloodbath. They were under the pay of wicked imperialist forces, and my job was to stop them. Afterwards, my heroism would have to go unnoticed because *The Incident*, which was the film's new title, would have to be kept top secret for fear of destabilising the community.

"I'm not sure my character would say that," I said, feeling that *Yellow Devils* was not quite correct, them being red.

Fizzy dismissed such squeamishness with a wave of his hand.

146

"And," I said, "is it possible that there is a problem with plagiarism? Didn't John Wayne say this in *The Shores of Iwo Jima?*"

The word *plagiarism* proved too difficult a concept for Fizzy. It was his film, so he could have people say whatever he wanted. He knew what the public wanted and they wanted mayhem, brilliantly shot.

I thought mayhem was definitely the right term, but I was not too certain about the brilliance of the shots. The camera was coming at me from a low angle and then from reverse high angles and then panning directly through my legs and swivelling around through flames and smoke and looking as if a very complicated time would happen in the cutting room. This was not Stirling's style of movie and I sensed that my character was reduced to body-parts in big close up, intertwined with things blowing apart in lots of fireworks.

"When they see this film," said Fizzy, "they will say, Stirling did the boring bits but Freddy Tang did the really good bits."

"Freddy?"

"Yeah, Fizzy's too stupid a name for a director."

Who was I to argue? I wanted out as quickly as possible and the sooner I did my bit, the less likelihood of accidentally being blown up or run over.

My part in the shoot then ended and my doubles took over for the more extraordinary acrobatics with gunmen bouncing from rooftop to rooftop, running vertically up apartment block walls and swinging from flagpole to flagpole, each one symbolically alternating the clouds of Heaven with the hot coals of Hell. The rain that would normally have stopped all production activity was merely incorporated into Fizzy's ever-expanding story-line and extraordinary dialogue:

"I am damn unsatisfied to be killed in this way."

"Fatty, you with your thick face have hurt my instep."

"It is because of gun wounds again."

"Damn, I'll burn you into a BBQ chicken!"

I was left quite breathless in my fear that Fizzy had not got a clue what he was really doing, and worse still, because of the high energy explosiveness of the events that he was concocting for the camera, it would not matter one little bit. This would either be heralded as one of the greatest creative endeavours

147

ever, or become a cult classic of such cheesy kitsch that either way everyone would laugh all the way to the bank.

If the writers of humanity ever got a whiff of what the directors of Hell were throwing together, they would despair. But on the other hand, a lot of the unusable, old fashioned, outrageous, mixed-up, bad-assed, confused and downright dull-dead and out-of-use-characters lingering in unfinished stories, unproduced scripts, half-baked novels, and one-night theatrical productions would come roaring back to life showing off what they can do when reality is arbitrary and all that matters is that you are caught between Heaven and Hell.

The ease with which I shrugged off my creative disquiet I put down to my newly acquired appreciation of the quality of humanity, or at least giant Kung Fu lizard men. There was the lack of need for perfection. There was the mere facility with what one did; and thus sheer verve and energy of execution mattered more than what was said. Since there was nothing worth saying that had not already been said better by ancient philosophers, one could not compete. It was thus better to merely imitate; and where one felt the spirit moved, one let it move as much as possible. This way no-one needed to sit and agonise. One went with the flow and all things came, as long as one did not want anything specific very badly.

Lily then! Should I give her up? Was it humane to continue with her? Was it really so bad that she was sixteen (just) and I was thirty? She often spoke like she was forty-six! She was smart. She was beautiful. She was rampant! Moreover, I would hate to hurt her. What was the wise thing to do? I could not think of anything wise to do and so I phoned her. Maybe I was hoping to declare my love. Or maybe say goodbye. Or maybe just to get one last fuck. There was no thought behind this process. There was nothing much to be gained either way. My motivation was just for the sake of a big finish.

I heard a gruff devilish voice on the end of the line. Maybe someone had stolen her phone and they were now in Hell making long distance phone-calls?

I decided to go round to her apartment and Mr Ng and Mr Kwok appeared out of a side street and followed me.

"I thought you were still required on set," I said.

"Ha ha ha," said both Mr Ng and Mr Kwok.

I was not certain why they were following me, but when I decided to try and hit the intercom on the door and tell Lily that I was there, they stood before me grinning.

"We can take you," said Mr Ng.

"Ha ha ha," said Mr Kwok.

I decided that I had better not discuss matters further. I walked on and pulled my phone out for another attempt. When I punched out Lily's number, I noticed that Mr Kwok reached inside his jacket, pulled out a phone and answered, "What?" at exactly the same time as the voice on my phone said, "What?" Then Mr Kwok waved at me and Mr Kwok and Mr Ng again did their best Kung Fu film laugh, only louder, and I got the message.

I thought I had better go and wait for Lily to contact me.

It was raining, the wind was coming in gusts, trees were beginning to shed branches, and overhead signs were beginning to swing a little precariously, so I escaped out of the weather into a restaurant. There I supped some noodles and wondered if she was locked in a room, chained to a bed and being fed nothing but congee. There were innumerable scenarios, none of which were very happy ones.

At first, I felt that I might forget about her. But if I were capable of empathy, if I were a human being, surely I would not let a young girl suffer like that? Or perhaps she was not suffering and my pursuing her was causing the suffering?

I went to find her grandfather. Maybe if I had no wisdom, he would supply it. He was old after all. But he was also just a deadbeat, old-hat stereotype, trapped in Hell. Even so, I felt the story, my story, needed this visit.

I was not sure of the name of the shop. It was somewhere in the back streets, which were not too few, but I had all afternoon so was bound to come across it.

I roamed the streets, buying yet another umbrella to add to my collection. I always forgot to bring one out with me and it always rained, so I always bought yet another thirty dollars' worth.

I was surprised by the emptiness of the streets even though I knew devils did not like the rain. This time, it was falling in thick glutinous warm drops that at least cleaned the air of its blue haze of smog. I could smell a mix of incense ash and boiling fat tumbling from the windows and doorways. Little funeral shops with lanterns, incense, paper models of aeroplanes and paper houses with paper servants darkly lined one street. I felt I must be getting close. A snake-meat shop, with a few snake gizzards on a blood-drenched chopping-board seemed to ring a bell. Then I saw the medicine shop with Lily's grandfather leaning against the door lintel. He was smoking a cigarette and watching the rain, then his attention strayed to me approaching. When I arrived at the doorway the old man did not budge but defied me to push by him if I wanted to come into the shop.

I asked if he had seen Lily recently. The old man grunted noncommittally. I persisted, causing the old man to grin. Then eventually he told me that she had gone to the airport with her mother and was flying to America. He told me I would have to be quick to see her because there was a typhoon on its way.

I thanked him and tried to hail a taxi.

In the rain the taxis melt. Those I found were lined up under the banyan trees sporting their out-to-lunch signs. I had heard that it was possible to bargain and offer double fares to off-duty drivers. Nevertheless, I could not find any. Rain meant a longer lunch break and money was of no interest.

I ran towards the harbour front where I knew a bus service ran. The clouds were darkening and I doubted that even Fizzy at his most megalomaniac could be filming under these circumstances. I hesitated a moment as I wondered if plane services were cancelled but saw the faint shadow of a jet rising over the horizon. Within the shadow of the mountains, the airport might be protected from this blustering storm. Maybe typhoons had to be a whole lot more than wet and windy to stop jets in Hell.

I caught a bus and relaxed for a moment. I reasoned that a happy end was bound to be the outcome. This was the last sequence in the movie. Whatever I thought, whatever I wanted to do, I was destined forever to make this run in the last reel.

I arrived at the airport and ran through the electric doors. The freezing cold of the air-conditioning took my breath away. I checked the TV screen. Which flight would she be on?

Crowds milled around: Indians, Chinese, Fillipinos, Thais, Taiwanese, laden down dragging red, blue and white striped plastic bags if they were poor, and nifty little trolleys if they were rich. It seemed a rule of the airport that the more money you had, the less luggage.

I tannoyed, asking Lily to phone the information desk if she had already passed through immigration. The phone on the desk rang and I grabbed it before the information officer could. I breathlessly announced that it was me on the phone.

"And this is Lily," she said.

"Whatever they told you isn't true," I said.

"They told me you'd left."

"Well I haven't."

"They told me you had a Filipina girlfriend who was pregnant."

"That's Sydney, not me!"

"I didn't believe them."

"Is your mother there?"

"Yes. She's not happy about this but I told her I would not get on the plane unless I spoke to you."

"Don't get on the plane."

She hesitated.

"What's there to think about?" I said. "Stay in Hell with me!"

As soon as I said it I knew it was stupid.

"I'm going with my mother. Maybe your writer will see me, and write someone like me into your story."

The phone went dead. I did not know whether I felt relief or sadness. I dripped onto the floor and folded up my umbrella. I braced myself to leave and searched the signs for exits. I seemed to wander about the airport for ages until I found the right door to the taxi ranks.

I wanted to destroy something. I wanted to kick in a plate glass window. I wanted to run through the streets with a machete hacking up anyone in my path. There were no words to describe what I felt. It was all bollocks, I decided. Everything was bollocks. It meant nothing. My love for Lily was bollocks. It was an aberration. The emotion came out of nothing. It was a fantasy. It was a trick of the mind. In real life, it never happens. This was just the fantasy that real lifers wanted to happen and I was doomed forever to be living it for the entertainment of the audience.

There would be no taxis now. There would be no buses either. All cars were told to get off the street. All planes were stopped. Windows were being taped up, sandbags were being laid at shop doors, and the wind was beginning to whip up into umbrella-destroying gusts. The airport officials called through their loudhailers saying that there would be no taxis. People began traipsing back into the airport to work out what would be the best thing to do.

Inside, tannoys announced the cancelling of flights. The airport flight indicators clacked and flapped like a falling pack of cards and showed *cancelled.* I stood and wondered what to do. Typhoons meant serious business as far as I was concerned. I had never experienced a typhoon before. I had seen films where they came and ripped up trees, tore down buildings and flooded everything in sight. Typhoons were a failure of the imagination. Nobody could be born when there was a typhoon in Hell.

Passengers began filing back into the passenger halls led by airhostesses carrying banners. Crowds of passengers were being assigned to various hotels for the night. I looked to see if I could see Lily. I could see Alice pulling her trolley. She was not happy. She looked this way and that. Padget trailed behind her and looked annoyed. I ran up to her.

"Where's Lily?" I asked.

"She's not with you then?" said Alice.

I shook my head and Alice looked around.

"Stupid girl!" she said. "I think she went looking for you. Why did you have to phone her? She was perfectly happy before you phoned."

"She wasn't!"

"Look she knew you were a shit so when we told her you'd gone, she accepted it."

"She wouldn't have done. She would have been very upset."

"She is now! So where is she?"

"I don't know?"

We left the airport and watched the rain.

"She can't be out here looking for you, can she?" said Alice.

I shook my head. I did not know.

For a moment, we watched the water rushing along the road outside the airport down into the drains.

"She'll have got a bus or something," said Alice. "She won't be walking. Where would she walk to?"

Padget began to get impatient. Alice snatched my phone and phoned up Fizzy.

"Get out there and look for her, you bastard!" she yelled at him.

"She didn't want to stay with me," said Fizzy. "She wanted to run off with that bastard."

"Hey!" I yelled, snatching the phone from Alice. "I heard that."

"Yeah you're lucky I finished the film with you after what I heard you were doing. That is more than a betrayal of trust. Greater men have found themselves in considerable distress for doing less to me."

"I did not do anything to you," I said. "And now your daughter is in danger."

"You're the one in danger."

"She could be anywhere."

"Go to the temple and we'll see," said Fizzy.

"What temple?"

Fizzy had already hung up.

*

I made Alice tell me where to go. She went with Padget to his mother's and wanted to be kept up to date on what was happening and whether her daughter would be accompanying her. She also warned me that if I hurt her she would kill me.

"Then you should also look for your daughter?"

"It's not in the script."

"Then, you are a turtle!"

I decided that characters who offered up lame excuses for their actions were the turtles, though I knew that in Hell there is no justice. Better characters were right that moment being washed out of their homes, along the gutters and down the drains into the mud of the turtle world. And maybe, that was where I was going.

There were no taxis though. I was hoping – for symmetrical story-structure purposes – that my favourite driver would appear out of the storm, click open the door and beckon me in. I would then be whisked through the floods, through the clouds, through the wind and rain and lightning, through the fissure in the rock

153

and taken to the hall. The girl would be dressed in red silk pyjamas with a red veil over her head awaiting me for a wedding before the black judge of Hell. But of course, that was someone else's story, not mine.

The street map I consulted dissolved in my hand as I thumbed through the soaked pages trying to find the small square where Fizzy's grandfather worshipped. When Lily was very young the grandfather used to take her there to have her fortune read. Normally only boys were taken for such things, but the old man had liked her and shown her things that he shouldn't. It did not matter though. Tradition was not to be taken too seriously. It was whatever kept the ghosts of the ancestors happy.

I found myself on one side of a road that had become a fierce river and on the other side was the small temple almost enclosed in a banyan tree. The temple was dirty, almost black with a coating of traffic exhaust. Some soggy paper dangled from the dripping half-dead tree with its stringy tendrils dangling from the branches to the ground where a blob of weathered stone coated in an offering of maggoty meat stood guard, having once been a lion.

I waded across, fighting against the current, to the other side of the road. I kicked away the broken syringes of the drug addicts that hung about the place late at night, and the rubbish blown onto the temple steps from the market. I looked in at the gloom where dingy gods cluttered up the altar. There was not much else inside apart from a rattan chair with a soggy newspaper strewn about its legs.

"Hello?" I said as I ventured inside. I stepped out of the way of the dripping roof and saw Lily shaking a small wooden bucket containing the yarrow stalks used in divination. More bollocks, I thought, but I stood reverentially as she shook a stick loose and her grandfather picked it up. He took it over to the old books that were kept screwed up among old instant-noodle pots and mouldering cigarette packets. Lily put her finger up to her lips to make sure that I said nothing as the old man put on his reading glasses and began reading the characters under the number that Lily had thrown.

"Does he see a dripping wet stranger who has travelled a long way to say he loves you?" I asked.

Lily shushed me.

Beside the wind, rain, thunder and lightning, a car could be heard sloshing through the water and sliding to a halt. I looked out. I could see it was Fizzy and his cronies arriving in a Mercedes. My heart sank. They did not look like they were going to be very friendly.

"It's your father," I said, disturbing Lily who was listening to her grandfather explaining how someone close to her was in mortal danger. With a deep sigh, she went to see and as soon as Fizzy caught sight of her, another car raced through the water, churning up a wave that soaked him. As he angrily turned to shout at the transgressor, explosions blew out of his chest. Blood shot into the air. Smoke belched from the window of the passing car that then sped off and disappeared into the thick swirling water with a hail of bullets chasing after it.

Fizzy staggered a moment and fell onto the temple steps. Lily knelt down beside him, stunned by what she had seen. I stepped forward, then back. I did not know whether to run or what. I grabbed Lily and tried to drag her away in case more gunfire was heading our way but she shook me off and began shaking Fizzy.

The grandfather ran out with a cushion and a blanket and snatched my phone from me since I seemed incapable of making any use of it. Lily found that Fizzy was still breathing and Fizzy opened his eyes as she cradled his head.

"You stay and look after the old man," said Fizzy.

"I will, I will," said Lily.

"And if I survive, you'll stay and look after me?"

"I will! I will!" she said tearfully.

One of his men snatched the phone from grandfather and stopped him making the call.

"He's phoning the hospital!" I said indignantly.

"No need," said Mr Kwok.

"We know what to do," said Mr Ng.

They lifted Fizzy up.

"You're not supposed to move him!" I said, beginning to think I should take control of this situation. "Tell them!" I said to Lily who did not know which way to turn.

Fizzy held up his hand and shook his head.

"We have people who know what to do."

Mr Ng and Mr Kwok took Fizzy by the legs and shoulders and carried him towards the Mercedes.

155

I glanced at the grandfather who was now standing with the blanket in his hand looking very serious, but there was something about this look that I could tell was more contempt than concern.

I knelt down and stuck my finger in the blood on the doorstep. I recognised this.

"It's fucking Kensington Gore. Purchased by the bucket from any theatrical suppliers!"

Lily did not know what that meant.

I pursued Fizzy and began prodding him. His men tried to shake me off.

"You're a fucking fraud!" I yelled, wrestling Mr Ng off Fizzy's feet and knocking them both to the floor. Fizzy and I struggled in the torrent of water.

"He's faking it!" I yelled.

Fizzy slowly sat up and stayed there on the floor with the rain beating down on him.

"It was a good ruse," said Fizzy. "And it would have worked perfectly."

Lily gave Fizzy a kick in the elbow and stormed off towards the temple.

Fizzy painfully fondled his elbow and sniffed a drip of water from the end of his nose.

"You can't do anything straight can you?" I said.

"Fack orf!" said Fizzy. "It could have worked."

"So you gambled on your own daughter's love," I said, remembering a line from one of my *West End Central* episodes.

Fizzy gave a shrug and climbed into his Mercedes and Mr Kwok and Mr Ng drove him away.

I went to fetch Lily but the grandfather stopped me.

"You don't understand," I said. "It's raining. This is the moment. This is when I find the no-name cat."

The grandfather shook his head and waved the book of fortune at me. It was apparently not good for me to go after her.

Nevertheless, I went, hoping to catch up by the pedestrian walkway. As I ran through the rain, I saw a mother and her young son wading across the fast-flowing water rushing along the gutter. Suddenly she stumbled and let go of the boy's hand. He slipped and rolled into the water that tumbled him over and over.

I ran to catch him. The boy slid along the gutter towards the storm drain. He looked too big to go down but then I saw his feet disappearing and leapt into the water, took the boy's arm, and was sucked with him into the drain but I stuck at the entrance. Slowly I inched the boy out with water flowing around him. The mother was screaming and then she grabbed the boy and pulled him free. I held on tight at the drain's entrance, fearing being sucked down. The water began flowing over my head. A turtle half swam, half swept along, hit me in the face. It farted.

"Sydney?"

"How on earth did you recognise me, old boy?"

"You're a turtle!"

"Always was at heart, I guess."

"But we're inextricably linked together as some mystical psychic all woollen twin set."

"That's right. And in Turtle Heaven everyone is exactly the same as each other. We'll be as one again."

"Is that good?"

"Nobody argues in Turtle Heaven. You wallow in the mud a bit. You get a bit of sun. You chew a bit of weed. You fuck."

"And you do a lot of stepping on each other's heads!"

"Nothing's perfect. Come on ... Come on ... Just let go. Just go with the flow. Just settle down into the sediment at the bottom ..."

*

I did not feel well the next day. I had drunk some drain water and it had given me diarrhoea. I was covered in bruises and scratches, all of which I was certain were about to burst into horrible sores at the slightest provocation. Nevertheless, I rose, showered, and pondered the previous day's events. I switched on the radio and heard an account of the storm damage. Characters swept to sea. Landslides, floods, road blockages and abandoned cars to be cleared out of the way before business could get back to normal. And a little story about me rescuing a youngster about to be swept down a storm drain.

Immediately there was a phone-call from the radio station asking me if I would be interviewed. I agreed and said I just happened to be passing by and saw the boy, so grabbed him. "Maybe if I'd known I was nearly going to get stuck down there myself I wouldn't have tried," I said. "But my ignorance most likely saved the boy."

"Great," said the interviewer. "Great line. Thanks."

I hung up, showered, and returned to some semblance of humanity. I went to a local restaurant for a quick breakfast bowl of congee. I supped, read my paper, watched the workers clearing away the tree debris, and took pleasure in the front page picture of me bedraggled and held up by a couple of firemen. I suddenly heard a jet overhead and realised that flights had begun again.

I phoned the airport and found out the flight times. I took a taxi to make sure I would be in time to say my goodbyes. The taxi-driver recognised me from my picture in the papers.

"Ah, very good," said the driver. "You are a human being now."

"Hardly," I said.

The driver's head nodded in time with the Buddha on the dashboard.

"Why," I asked, "is Buddhist kitch so much cooler than Christian or Muslim or Jewish junk?"

"Are you asking me that as a neo-post-modern deconstructionalist or as a guy who drives a taxi?"

"A taxi-driver."

"Because he's a funny little fat guy with an air-freshener built in."

CHAPTER EIGHT

At the Airport I met up with Lily and Alice.

"I'm staying," said Lily. "But not with you. You've other things happening to you."

"You're not staying with your father then?"

"I'll stay with my grandfather. There's so many battles to be fought before I can leave."

"You're going to introduce Hell to the concept of protest are you?"

"I'm going to see what emerges. Maybe I'll get rich instead and become one of the custodians of Hell."

Alice nodded acknowledgement; she had made a quick killing on Hell shares and prudently pulled out before the peak. Four hundred percent in three months was not bad going.

Fizzy arrived with his arm in a sling, and a massive display of flowers.

"I'm going before he starts," said Lily, giving me a kiss and then her mother. She walked past Fizzy.

"She'll come round," he said as he watched Lily heading towards the taxis, "when she needs some money."

"I don't think that's the answer," said Alice, taking the flowers. "But, for what it's worth. There were moments, weren't there."

Fizzy nodded.

"There were moments. If Padget causes you trouble, just let me know."

Alice grinned and Padget scowled as they walked towards emigration.

"I guess things turned out OK," said Fizzy. "In a way."

"In a way," I agreed.

"Me and Lily, we'll get written by some Chinese writers now. We won't be just some exotic colouring with funny accents. And that's good."

Fizzy and I listened to the sound of the airport. We watched a bevy of news reporters with their leather bags heading off to pastures new.

"We're no longer news to your guys," said Fizzy. "They won't care what happens here. None of you people."

"I might," I said.

"No," said Fizzy. "You've been here now. It's time to go somewhere else. Like me. Time for me to go somewhere else, too."

"Hollywood for you is it? Bollywood? Hong Kong?"

"We'll see. We'll see. Keep in touch. Me and you, we're horns of the same goat."

"We're not actually."

"It's a good line though."

Fizzy limped off and looked a little sad as far as I could tell.

"It's a lousy line," I shouted and I could swear he shrugged.

There is always a moment as one settles into an aircraft when the engines are humming, when the earphones are hissing, and the stomach is a little tense as the plane leans back and makes its leap into the sky, when one feels that one is going somewhere. The moment fades away and one is merely on a plane and facing the prospect of sitting in an uncomfortable seat for seventeen hours. Going somewhere just becomes a journey from A to B, where one had the unfortunate inconvenience of having some business to be done that could not be done over the phone.

At least I had some business. I was a character in a new TV series. I also had a new writer, though I did not really trust a girl whose main source of inspiration was old TV episodes; but if I am worth recycling, then I must have something redeemable about me.

I flicked through the personal TV channels to see what was on. I was gratified to see that there were no ancient repeats of *West End Central*. I could at least settle down and forget my public ... what public? I couldn't care less ... I took out my journal and went to scribble down a few musings about the messiness of life and how its complications are simplified by the media and misrepresented. Only early death produces heroes. Only death can sanctify. Age with its compromises, the follies of one's emotions, mistakes and fallibility, cannot then tarnish one with humanity.

What sort of character had I become? I wondered, and shuddered because I could see life was always going to be tough for me.

I felt a tap on my shoulder and looked around to see Cherry Halligan. She asked if the seat beside me was free. I was rather hoping no-one would take it since I would have a little extra room to stretch out. Cherry did not await an answer but sat beside me and ordered a gin and tonic.

"I like the beard," she said. "It covers that scar, but you'll never be able to do drag again."

"Is that a great loss?"

"Probably not," she said, pulling out her portable cassette recorder and sitting it on the table before her. "I saw the news about you doing your heroic bit."

"I just happened to be there."

"You wouldn't have got me leaping into that filth," she said giving a good slurp on the gin.

"I thought you went home a couple of weeks ago."

"Last minute re-writes. Touch and go."

Cherry switched on her tape-recorder and smiled.

"Is this an interview?"

"Yeah," she said, "You got any objections?"

"Would you sleep with me for this?"

"I tell you what: tonight that's exactly what I'll do. Me and the rest of the passengers."

As the airliner rattled into the air, luggage jumping about the storage cupboards, condensation dripping from the ceiling, the seat belt sign flickering on and off, I turned to watch the fires of Hell burning in the night. I thought I saw a familiar face look in through the porthole; a windswept face with a booze-laden nose sweatily smearing the glass and grinning at me. I leaned closer to peer out of the window and saw Sydney clinging to the engine, the fires of the jet flashing and rumbling as they singed the seat of Sydney's pants.

"But I thought you were a turtle," I muttered to myself. But then I guess that would have been too much of a downer. People always like the Sydneys. Somehow, they want them to exist despite their never amounting to much. That is all that any of us are really. We are creatures that others would like to exist because we entertain them, and sometimes we enlighten them. Our sufferings are safe; our thrills are without spills. And our entertainment is the history of the lives we pretend to have.

I clasped Cherry's hand tightly and asked, "What do you want to know about me, exactly?"

AFTERWORD

Cop Show Heaven does it all wrong—on purpose.

I wrote that previous sentence, the first sentence, my hook, three times before settling on the em-dash in order to highlight the qualification "on purpose." I first wrote: *Cop Show Heaven* does it all wrong on purpose." Then: "*Cop Show Heaven* does it all wrong. On purpose." So why, finally, the em-dash? Maybe so that I could display my knowledge of the not-widely-known term for that type of punctuation mark? Yet doing so—didactically parading—also makes me pretentious. But doesn't the self-reflexive admission of this flaunting, of this pomposity performance, somehow redeem me, somehow make me honest—and perhaps, and this perversely, even kind of likeable, especially given my moderating qualifiers?

I read Lawrence Gray's *Cop Show Heaven* as a sustained meditation on the concerns I've just raised, namely, narrative, performance, honesty, reflexivity, and individuality. Here's my favorite paragraph from Gray's very smart parody of a parody of police-themed TV shows in handover-era (a *zeitgeist* we still inhabit) Hong Kong:

> One of the things sitting uneasily in my mind was the kind of label I should attach to my newly acquired genre. Was I a liberal democrat because I tut-tutted these attacks on civil liberties, or was I a rabid old fascist because I thought the media was over doing the panic in the streets scenario for crass commercial or sleazy self serving racist motives? Was there not now a tinge of heavenly colonialism in my thought processes? Or was this a post colonial liberal cosmopolitan outlook that denied nationalistic claims upon cities and proclaimed them as belonging to those that lived there and contributed to their culture? Should I applaud the localisation of the civil service on the one hand, but deplore the moves to make sin compulsory? Was this political thriller I coveted developing serious didactic pretensions and reducing its chances of popularity?

The answer to this series of serious, and necessary, rhetorical questions is: *all of the above.* Such is the fate of the institutionally threatened individual in contemporary Hong Kong. And elsewhere. Questions. Questions with always already (i) incomplete, (ii) dishonest, (iii) defeatist, (iv) propagandistic, (v) racialist, (vi) masculinist, (vii) paranoid, and/or (viii) self-condemning responses.

Let me backtrack.

Parody of a parody of police-themed TV shows?

On the face of it, Cop Show Heaven becomes Cop Show Hell post-handover. Gray does not even disguise this Hong Kong-good vs China-bad dialectic. Instead, he critiques said simplicity to great effect by demonstrating how the legally sanctioned erosion of civil liberties is ongoing, is pervasive. One can almost as easily see *Cop Show Heaven* as an ironical allegory of Czechoslovakia's Velvet Revolution or apply it as a topical allegory of the Ferguson Protests. Or, better: read it as an analog to Hong Kong's very recent Umbrella Movement; a protest literally polarizing pro-democratic activists and laissez-faire capitalists. (Umbrellas are pervasive in *Cop Show Heaven*. But, then again, they seem always to have been so in Tropic of Cancer Hong Kong.) As first-person narrator Dan Symmonds laments, "Take away their vote and no-one gives a damn but take away their mobiles ...Ooo, now there is trouble."

Still, parody of a parody?

Hong Kong's well-recognized as a mecca of police- or detective-themed drama. Think of Lau and Mak's *Infernal Affairs* (2002), the celebrated source of Scorcese's Academy Award for Best Film *The Departed* (2006). Think too of HK's *Exiled*, *PTU*, *Mad Detective*, and *Kill Zone*. Or even of Wong Kar-wei's *Chungking Express* and *In the Mood for Love*, the former starring a cop and drug smuggler, the latter focusing on affairs, secrets, and detection. But along with the good, so the saying goes, comes the bad. (This idiom is perhaps particularly *a propos* in the context of a Hong Kong where cops hide their badges and beat students and journalists, of a Hong Kong where the law appears increasingly suspect, if not outright unlawful.) And Gray skillfully parodies bad filmic representation by making a virtue of accentuating that which differentiates the adroit (the good) from the clumsy (the bad).

This is Gray's hitch; this is the one degree of remove or regression that makes *Cop Show Heaven* a parody of a parody:

Gray deftly makes his good novel look bad. The author finds refuge in a form of honesty that isn't afraid to expose its fictionality. To put it differently, Gray shows that realism is never realism *tout court*. Rather, realism is *in media res*, is in process, is an endless editing only ever arbitrarily representative when the corporate deadline intersects, when the media machine, all but destined to do so, takes over. Overtakes. Manipulates. Determines. Is.

Our narrator is Dan Symmonds, whose name appears variously with and without the double "m." Gray accentuates this intentional error when Dan incorrectly corrects the misspelling of his name in a newspaper: "Dan Simons, (sic) disgraced TV character, finds his own level." The *sic erat scriptum*, of course, is not a comma splice, as the "(sic)" erroneously points out, but instead, the spelling of our antihero's name as "Simons." (The correction should read: "Dan Simons [sic], disgraced TV character, finds his own level.") Dan Sym(m)onds' nemesis is the unlikeable and (or because?) underdeveloped Padgett, whose name appears throughout the text both with and without the second "t." Intentional errors of continuity, as well as of anachronism, likewise recur. Dan has no phone. He receives a phone-call. Dan is *in absentia* from the Lolita-modelled Lily for two weeks. He misses her birthday which was a month away. Dan wonders if the airport, "Within the shadow of the mountains," "might be protected from this blustering storm." The old Kai Tak airport, however, was in an urban center. The new Chek Lap Kok airport, nestled among Lantau's high hills, does not open until July 1998, a full year after the handover. Responding to the taxi-driver's "Maybe you get too much sun?"(a "taxi-driver" who is also Scorcese's "Taxi Driver"), Dan overtly "recall[s] Shakespeare's Hamlet" as he retorts "Ah, it is that I am in the sun too much." The line in *Hamlet*, however, actually reads "I am too much in the sun." *Hamlet* likewise appears in the form of the interchangeable Guildenstern and Rosencrantz derived henchmen Mr Ng and Mr Kwok.

Mere quibbles? Perhaps. But this, I think, is Gray's point. How to demarcate any definitive line in the sand, any conclusive identity, or genre, or periodization? How to instruct without being didactic? How to delight without being flippant? How to discriminate without being prejudiced? How to critique without being disparaging? How to respect without being obsequious? How to be self-reflective without being narcissistic? How to represent without being reductive? How to be a self when we're all so hybridized? How to be at all when we're all still, still, still, still, becoming? And the existential problem is all the more complex for *Cop Show Heaven*'s Dan. A Pirandello figure, a character in search of an author—Dan lingers in the wings waiting to be written, to be interpellated, into a novel narrative, a fresh set of conventions, *un nouveau régime*, a new "normal."

Jason S Polley
Associate Professor
Hong Kong Baptist University

Author of *Refrain* (Proverse 2010), *Cemetery Miss You* (Proverse 2011), and *Jane Smiley, Jonathan Franzen, Don DeLillo: Narratives of Everyday Justice* (Lang 2011).

ADVANCE RESPONSE

Fancy a novel of ideas? Now, don't be frightened. This isn't Gaardner; more Pynchon, actually. It's just that everyone in *Cop Show Heaven* is only a concept. They're stock heroes, heavies and hookers from TV cop shows who are "between projects". They've been written out of the script and are waiting to be written into another so they can be reincarnated by a real live actor, preferably in a Hollywood film, but more realistically in a series on Thai TV. Meanwhile they're stuck in a sort of limbo—cop show heaven—that remarkably resembles turn-of-the-century Hong Kong.

Here is Hong Kong's handover from Britain to China as it has never been seen before, in an absurd, allegorical fantasy that will have anyone familiar with the place laughing from beginning to end. Nothing is spared: the British, the communists, the gangsters, kung fu, traditional Chinese medicine, religion in all its forms. The send-ups are endless. Hong Kong itself is a bit of hell rented by heaven to allow deceased directors to continue making films. This being heaven, God gets a walk-on part, speaking British slang, no less.

Hong Kong as heaven! Now you've seen it all. Weird? Yes, but this is a great piece of writing and great fun to read. It's a *tour de force*. I don't know what this dude Gray is smoking, but where can I get some?

Bill Purves
Author of six works of non-fiction

ABOUT PROVERSE HONG KONG

Proverse Hong Kong is based in Hong Kong with long-term and expanding regional and international connections.

Proverse has published novels, novellas, fictionalized autobiography, non-fiction (including autobiography, biography, history, memoirs, sport, travel narratives), single-author poetry collections, children's, teens / young adult and academic books. Other interests include diaries, and academic works in the humanities, social sciences, cultural studies, linguistics and education. Some Proverse books have accompanying audio texts. Some are translated into Chinese.

Proverse welcomes authors who have a story to tell, wisdom, perceptions or information to convey, a person they want to memorialize, a neglect they want to remedy, a record they want to correct, a strong interest that they want to share, skills they want to teach, and who consciously seek to make a contribution to society in an informative, interesting and well-written way. Proverse works with texts by non-native-speaker writers of English as well as by native English-speaking writers.

The name, "Proverse", combines the words "prose" and "verse" and is pronounced accordingly.

THE PROVERSE PRIZE

The Proverse Prize, an annual international competition for an unpublished book-length work of fiction, non-fiction, or poetry, was established in January 2008. It is open to all who are at least eighteen on the date they sign the entry form. Unusually for a competition of this nature, there is no restriction based on nationality, residence or citizenship.

The objectives of the Proverse Prize are: to encourage excellence and / or excellence and usefulness in publishable written work in the English Language, which can, in varying degrees, "delight and instruct". Entries are invited from anywhere in the world. Semi-finalists to date include writers born or resident in Andorra, Australia, Canada, Germany, Hong Kong, New Zealand, Nigeria, Singapore, South Africa, Taiwan, The Bahamas, the Peoples' Republic of China, the United Arab Emirates, the United Kingdom, the USA.

Founders: Verner Bickley and Gillian Bickley. To celebrate their lifelong love of words in all their forms as readers, writers, editors, academics, performers, and publishers.

Honorary Legal Advisor: Mr Raymond T. L. Tse.

Honorary Accountant: Mr Neville Chow.

Honorary Judges: Anonymous.

Honorary Advisors: Bahamian poet Marion Bethel; UK translator, Margaret Clarke; UK linguist & lexicographer David Crystal; Canadian poet and academic, Jonathan Hart; Swedish linguist Björn Jernudd; Hong Kong University Librarian, Peter Sidorko; Singapore poet Edwin Thumboo; Czech novelist & poet Olga Walló.

Honorary UK agent and distributor: Christine Penney

Honorary Administrators: Proverse Hong Kong.

Proverse Prize Winners Whose Books Have Already Been Published By Proverse Hong Kong

Laura Solomon, Rebecca Jane Tomasis, Gillian Jones, David Diskin, Peter Gregoire, Sophronia Liu, Birgit Linder, James McCarthy, Celia Claase, Philip Chatting.

Summary Terms and Conditions
(for indication only & subject to revision)

The information below is for guidance only. Please refer to the year-specific Proverse Prize Entry Form & Terms & Conditions, which are uploaded in April each year onto the Proverse Hong Kong website: <www.proversepublishing.com>.

The free Proverse E-Newsletter includes ongoing information about the Proverse Prize. To be put on the E-Newsletter mailing-list, email: info@proversepublishing.com with your request.

The Prize
1) Publication by Proverse Hong Kong, with
2) Cash prize of HKD10,000 (HKD7.80 = approx. US$1.00)

Supplementary publication grants may be made to selected other entrants for publication by Proverse Hong Kong.

Depending on the quality of the work in any year, the prize may be shared by at most two entrants or withheld, as recommended by the judges.

In 2015, the entry fee was: HKD220.00 OR GBP32.00.

Writers are eligible, who are at least eighteen on the date they sign The Proverse Prize entry documents. There is no nationality or residence restriction.

Each submitted work must be an unpublished publishable single-author work of non-fiction, fiction or poetry, the original work of the entrant, and submitted in the English language. School textbooks and plays are ineligible.

Translated work: If the work entered is a translation from a language other than English, both the original work and the translation should be previously unpublished. The submitted work will not be judged as a translation but as an original work.

Extent of the Manuscript: within the range of what is usual for the genre of the work submitted. However, it is advisable that novellas be in the range 30,000 to 45,000 words); other fiction (e.g. novels, short-story collections) and non-fiction (e.g. autobiographies, biographies, diaries, letters, memoirs, essay collections, etc.) should be in the range, 75,000 to 100,000 words. Poetry collections should be in the range, 5,000 to 25,000 words. Other word-counts and mixed-genre submissions are not ruled out.

Writers may choose, if they wish, to obtain the services of an Editor in presenting their work, and should acknowledge this help and the nature and extent of this help in the Entry Form.

KEY DATES FOR THE PROVERSE PRIZE
IN ANY YEAR
(subject to confirmation and/or change)

Receipt of Entry Fees / Entry Documents	[Varies but no later than] 14 April to 31 May of the year of entry
Receipt of entered manuscripts	1 May to 30 June of the year of entry
Announcement of semi-finalists	July-September of the year of entry
Announcement of finalists	October-December of the year of entry
Announcement of winner/ max two winners (sharing the cash prize)	December of the year of entry to April of the year that follows the year of entry
Cash Award made	At the same time as publication of the work(s) adjudged the winner / joint-winners of the Proverse Prize
Publication of winning work(s)	In or after November of the year that follows the year of entry

NOVELS, SHORT STORY COLLECTIONS
AND OTHER FICTION
Published by Proverse Hong Kong

If you have enjoyed Lawrence Gray's *Cop Show Heaven* , you may also enjoy his short story collection, *Odds and Sods*.

**You may also like to read the following
(all titles in English unless otherwise stated)**

A Misted Mirror, by Gillian Jones. 2011.
A Painted Moment, by Jennifer Ching. 2010.
An Imitation of Life, by Laura Solomon. 2013.
Article 109, by Peter Gregoire. 2012.
Bao Bao's Odyssey: from Mao's Shanghai to Capitalist Hong Kong, by Paul Ting. 2012.
Black Tortoise Winter, by Jan Pearson. Scheduled 2015 / 2016.
Bright Lights and White Nights, by Andrew Carter. 2015.
cemetery miss you, by Jason S Polley. 2011.
Cop Show Heaven, by Lawrence Gray. 2015.
Death has a Thousand Doors, by Patricia Grey. 2011.
Hilary and David, by Laura Solomon. 2011.
Instant Messages, by Laura Solomon. 2010.
Man's Last Song, by James Tam. 2013.
Mila the Magician, by Zhang Jian. 2013. (English / Chinese bilingual)
Mishpacha – Family, by Rebecca Tomasis. 2010.
Odds and Sods, by Lawrence Gray. 2013.
Paranoia (the Walk and Talk with Angela), by Caleb Kavon. 2012.
Red Bird Summer, by Jan Pearson. 2014.
Revenge from Beyond, by Dennis Wong. 2011.
The Day They Came, by Gérard Louis Breissan. 2012.
The Devil You know, by Peter Gregoire. 2014.
The Monkey in Me: Confusion, Love and Hope under a Chinese Sky, by Caleb Kavon. 2009.
The Monkey in Me, by Caleb Kavon. Translated by Chapman Chen. 2010. E-book. 2010. (Chinese)
The Perilous Passage of Princess Petunia Peasant, by Victor Edward Apps. 2014.

The Reluctant Terrorist: in Search of the Jizo, by Caleb Kavon. 2011.

The Shingle Bar Sea Monster and Other Stories, by Laura Solomon. 2012.

The Snow Bridge and Other Stories, by Philip Chatting. Scheduled 2015.

Tiger Autumn, by Jan Pearson. 2015.

The Village in the Mountains, by David Diskin. 2012.

Tightrope! A Bohemian Tale, by Olga Walló. Translated from Czech by Johanna Pokorny, Veronika Revická & others. 2010.

Tightrope! A Bohemian Tale, by Olga Walló. Translated by Chapman Chen. 2011. (Chinese)

University Days, by Laura Solomon. 2014.

Vera Magpie, by Laura Solomon. 2013.

OTHER GENRES

We also publish in other genres, including autobiography, biography, children's illustrated books, educational books, Hong Kong educational and legal history, memoirs, poetry, teenage / young adult books, and travel. Other genres may be added.

WRITE TO US!

We are interested to read your response to
Lawrence Gray's *Cop Show Heaven*
and any other of our publications.
Please write to our email address, proverse@netvigator.com,
giving us a few sentences which you are willing for us to
publish,
giving your comments on this book.
If what you write is chosen to be included
in our E-Newsletter or website,
we will select another title published by Proverse
and send you a complimentary copy.
Please include your name, email address and mailing address
when you write to us, and state whether or not we may cut or
edit your comments for publication.
We will use your initials to attribute your comments.

FIND OUT MORE ABOUT OUR AUTHORS AND BOOKS

Visit our website
http://www.proversepublishing.com

Visit our distributor's website
<www.chineseupress.com>

Follow us on Twitter
Follow news and conversation: <twitter.com/Proversebooks>
OR
Copy and paste the following to your browser window and follow the instructions: https://twitter.com/#!/ProverseBooks

'Like us' on Facebook: www.facebook.com/ProversePress

Request our E-Newsletter
Send your request to info@proversepublishing.com.

Availability
Most titles are available in Hong Kong and world-wide
from our Hong Kong based Distributor,
The Chinese University Press of Hong Kong,
The Chinese University of Hong Kong, Shatin, NT,
Hong Kong SAR, China. Email: cup-bus@cuhk.edu.hk

All titles are available from Proverse Hong Kong
and the Proverse Hong Kong UK-based Distributor.

We have stock-holding retailers in Hong Kong,
Singapore (Select Books), Canada (Elizabeth Campbell Books),
Principality of Andorra (Llibreria La Puça, La Llibreria).

Orders can be made from bookshops in the UK and elsewhere.

Ebooks
Most of our titles are available also as Ebooks.